ROSWELL
HIGH

THE INTRUDER

by

MELINDA METZ

D0620339

POCKET
BOOKS

An imprint of Simon & Schuster UK Ltd. A Viacom Company
Africa House, 64-78 Kingsway, London WC2B 6AH

Produced by 17th Street Productions, Inc.,
33 West 17th Street, New York, NY 10011

A CIP catalogue record for this book is available from the British Library

ISBN 07434 08829

1 3 5 7 9 10 8 6 4 2

Printed by Caledonian International Book Manufacturing, Glasgow
First published in USA in 1998 by Archway Paperbacks.

"Please, Max," a voice begged. "You can't die on me now . . . not after you finally agreed to be more than 'just friends.'"

The voice sounded so far away. Like it was coming from the end of a long tunnel. Max Evans turned in a slow circle. He didn't see anyone. He didn't see *anything,* anything but the light. The pure white light.

"The communication crystals are in your hand," the voice told him. "You have to connect to the collective consciousness, Max. Do it now! You don't have much time!"

The collective consciousness. That sounded familiar. Sort of. The voice sounded familiar, too. But he couldn't remember from where.

Max sat down, then stretched out on his back. The light was so awesome. It actually had patterns in it, like white snowflakes against white sheets or something. He just wanted to lie there and watch the bright snowflakes coming down.

New voices joined the first one. He felt as if he'd heard them before, too, a long time ago. All the voices joined together, pleading with him to make the connection. Join the consciousness. Live.

Max tried to tune them out. The snowflakes were something that should be looked at in silence. He didn't know how he knew that, but he did.

"Max, no! Don't die! You can't die. If you really love me, you'll stay with me," the first voice cried.

Liz. Liz Ortecho. The name appeared in big amber letters in his brain. How could he have forgotten the sound of Liz's voice, the voice of the girl he loved?

Now he recognized the other voices, too. His sister, Isabel's. And the voices of his friends Alex Manes and Maria DeLuca. He peered into the white light. Where were they?

Where was *he?*

"Can't see . . . ," he mumbled. He swallowed hard, trying to unglue his tongue from the roof of his mouth. "Where . . . where are you?"

"We're right here, Max. We're all here with you," Liz exclaimed. "Stay with us. Stay with me."

And without thinking about it, without deciding to do it, Max was up on his feet. Flying through the brilliant white light, the snowflakes whizzing past him faster and faster until they were nothing but blurs.

Then the light began to fade, and he could see he was speeding down a tunnel. His bed stood at the end, so far away it looked as tiny as a box of matches. Liz, Isabel, Alex, and Maria, small as dolls, gathered close around it, staring down at Max's body.

My body, Max thought. How can that be my body?

He was rushing straight toward the body on the bed until he was so close, he could see the droplets of sweat on the body's forehead, see the tiny splotches of blood on the body's lips. Then he slammed into the body—*his* body—and melded with it. He could feel the sheets crumpled beneath him. The pillow soft under his head. The air rasping in his lungs as he breathed. Liz's hand holding his.

"Focus on the crystals, Max. Connect to the collective consciousness," Liz urged.

The collective consciousness. This time the words brought back a rush of memory. He was going through his *akino,* his life change ceremony. If he didn't connect with the collective consciousness of his home planet, he would die.

And he'd thought that was what was going to happen because he couldn't make the connection without the communication crystals stored on his parents' spaceship. The ship kept in a secret compound, surrounded by guards with machine guns.

He turned his head slightly, locking eyes with Isabel. "You found the ship?" he asked his sister, his voice cracking. But he already knew the answer. He held the communication crystals in his hand. That was the proof. "Where's Michael?" he croaked out. "Ray?" They'd gone into the compound with Isabel, so they should be here, too.

"Not now," Isabel answered, her voice tight. "Make the connection, Max. Hurry!"

Liz pressed Max's fingers more tightly around the crystals. He closed his eyes, and he reached out with his mind. Instantly he felt, not a touch exactly, but the sensation of someone standing very close to him, close enough that the edges of their auras blended. It wasn't Liz, Isabel, Alex, or Maria. He knew the feel of their auras almost as well as he knew his own, and the aura touching his was unfamiliar . . . but somehow comforting.

Another *presence* moved close, its aura touching Max's, too, mixing with his, mixing with the aura of the first presence, until a single shared aura formed around the three of them. He felt none of the brain-shredding pain he'd experienced when he tried to connect to the collective consciousness without the crystals. This time connecting was like stepping into a tropical ocean, with the warm salty water surrounding him, making his body light and buoyant, rocking him with gentle waves.

The ocean was made of auras. Not just the two blended with his, but thousands of them. Hundreds of thousands of them. Maybe more.

Maybe millions. Max stretched out and out with his mind and could find no end.

He heard a single word from the two presences closest to him. The word wasn't spoken in English. It wasn't actually spoken at all. It was as if the essence of the word washed over his brain, needing no translation. *Son.*

Son. The word swept through Max again and again, filling him with emotions not his own. Joy and grief. Pride and longing. Love.

My parents. No. It can't be.

Yes, they answered without words. Yes, son.

But his parents . . . his parents were dead. They died when their spaceship crashed in the desert—the so-called Roswell Incident. They had been dead more than forty years when Max and Isabel broke free of their incubation pods.

So that meant he wasn't only connecting with all those who lived on his home planet. He was connecting to the spirits of the dead as well. Max felt his eyes start to burn. This just blew him away. His parents. He was actually communicating with his parents. He never thought . . . never even hoped . . .

An image flashed through his mind. Two shining beings staring down at the incubation pod Max shared with his sister. He felt a rush of the beings' giddy, practically giggly excitement, their eagerness to see their children born.

5

But they never had.

Max felt a stab of grief from his parents, a grief he was also experiencing himself. Then music began to play, humming, almost vibrating music, more like the sound a finger makes rubbing around the rim of a crystal glass than any musical instrument Max knew. It was a lullaby. The lullaby his mother's mother had sung for her, the one his mother had planned to sing to her children. This knowledge was somehow passed along to Max as he listened.

A new presence touched Max's aura, and the image of two moons, half covered by acid green clouds, filled his mind. Seconds later another new presence touched him, and a sweet, tangy liquid poured down his throat. It tasted exactly right, the way no earth food ever did. Max was always having to mix mouthwash into his orange soda or pickle juice into his milk to get them to taste good to him. But this—more of the liquid filled his mouth—this was perfect just the way it was.

Again a new presence touched Max, and a lemony, peppery smell enveloped him. With the smell came the knowledge that the scent belonged to a kind of berry that could be used to treat digestive problems.

They're each sharing a little scrap of information about my planet, Max thought. This was too cool.

Another presence touched him. He recognized

the aura instantly. It belonged to Ray Iburg, Max's boss at the UFO museum, and the only adult who had survived the crash. "Ray!" Max cried, not sure if he was actually using his vocal cords to shout the name or just his brain. "Ray, you saved my life. You, and Michael, and Isabel! I never thought you guys would make it back with the communication crystals in time! I don't even know what to say, how to thank you. All I know is we're going to have to have a serious party—maybe at the museum after we close tomorrow night."

An image filled Max's brain, an image of him and Ray in the museum, both dressed in the goofy sequined Elvis outfits Ray had had made, both laughing so hard, their faces were all scrunched up.

Ray was showing him one of the great times they'd had together. But the emotion Max was getting off Ray didn't match the picture. He wasn't getting anything close to laughter. There was relief, and sadness, and something that felt like a good-bye.

Another presence touched Max, breaking his connection with Ray. The image of the control panel of a spaceship replaced the image of Max and Ray. Knowledge about the mechanics of the panel filled his brain. Max tried to shove it away. He needed to connect with Ray again. What was going on with him? Why was there all that sadness pulsing off him?

"Ray!" Max called. "Where are you?"

Another new presence touched Max, and the sound of a low clacking surrounded him. With the sound came information—the clacking was a warning that a poisonous insect was nearby.

Max didn't care about that right now. "Ray!" he shouted. But there was no answer. Something was wrong. Something was very wrong.

Max opened his fingers, allowing the communication crystals to fall free of his hand. He could still feel the presences around him. Another one touched him, showing him the image of a being changing shape as it stepped out of a spaceship.

"Stop! Just stop!" Max yelled. He sat up in bed and immediately turned to his sister. "Isabel, tell me what happened to Ray," he demanded.

"Are you okay?" Liz cried. She pressed her palm against his forehead. "You look so much better. Are you—"

Max didn't take his eyes off Isabel. "I'm fine," he interrupted. "I just need to know what happened to Ray."

The devastated expression on Isabel's face told him everything. But he still needed to hear it.

"He's dead. Sheriff Valenti shot him," Isabel answered. "Ray was trying to save me, and Valenti shot him." Tears welled up in her blue eyes, and she wiped them away with a vicious sweep of her hand.

Liz sat down on the bed and pulled Max close

to her. He could tell from her breathing that she was trying not to cry. "I knew," Max whispered against her shoulder, the wool of her sweater making tiny scratches across his cheek. "I knew. That's why he was saying good-bye."

"What about Michael?" Maria asked, her voice quaking.

Max jerked up his head. Michael?

"The last time I saw him, he was fighting off a couple of guards," Isabel answered. Max could tell she was working hard to keep the emotion out of her voice. Michael Guerin was like a second brother to her. And to Max.

"And you left him there?" Maria cried, her voice climbing into a shriek.

"That's right. I left him there." Isabel's words came out hard and clipped. "I knew there was a chance he would survive on his own. But there was no way Max was going to live if I didn't get back here with the crystals."

Max felt the acid in his stomach start to bubble. Isabel had sacrificed Michael for him. If she'd stayed and helped him take out the guards, would Michael—

"He could still be alive," Liz said, pulling him away from this thoughts. "We've got to get out there right now. We've got to—"

"No," Alex interrupted. "They'll be expecting us. We'd never make it in."

"You're saying we should just leave him there?" Max demanded. There was no way that was happening.

"No, we won't leave him there," Alex shot back, obviously peeved. "But we have to make a plan, let a little time go by so we can catch them when they're not standing at the front door with an arsenal."

"I don't care what the rest of you do. I'm going to the compound. Now." Maria turned toward the door.

"Wait. I'm going with you," Max answered.

Alex moved to block the door. "Actually, neither of you is going anywhere." He turned to Isabel. "You said Michael was fighting off a couple of guards. That means they weren't using their machine guns on him, right?"

Machine guns, Max thought. Is that what Valenti used on Ray? A machine gun? Max tried not to imagine Ray's body jerking while the bullets hit.

"They were using . . ." Isabel swallowed. "I think they were cattle prods. Something that gave an electrical charge."

"Okay, so they must not want him dead," Alex continued. "Best-case scenario, he got away and is heading back here. Worst-case scenario, he's being held prisoner. But alive. We need to give him a little time to show up. If he doesn't, we'll make plans, and we'll get him out."

"Alex is right," Isabel said. "We go in now, it's over for all of us. If we wait until they're not expecting us, we at least have a shot."

"All right. I hate the thought of leaving Michael in there. But I think we have to do it," Liz agreed.

Alex glanced from Maria to Max. "You two, promise that you won't do anything stupid. No one goes to the compound before we come up with a strategy to get us all back out alive."

"Yeah, yeah. Okay. But we better come up with this brilliant strategy real soon," Max said.

Maria hesitated. "I'm with Max," she finally said. Then she shoved past Alex and bolted.

"Do you all mind just leaving me alone for a while? I'm really wiped out," Max said. It wasn't true. Connecting to the collective consciousness had left him feeling strong and invigorated. But he needed time to think, to process.

Ray was dead. Michael was captured. And it was all Max's fault. They wouldn't have been in the compound if he hadn't gotten sick.

He couldn't do anything about Ray. But he could do something about Michael. Yeah, he might wait a few days. But he would free Michael.

No matter what it took.

Michael Guerin paced around his cell, studying the glass walls. Well, what looked like glass walls. They were probably made of something a lot stronger. But not strong enough to keep him in if he really wanted to get out. Molecules were molecules. He could crush some of those molecules together and make a nice hole, one big enough for him to stroll through without even ducking his head.

But there was a problem. Make that two problems—two guards with machine guns and those cattle prods or whatever they were. If there were only one, Michael would have taken a shot at busting out. Yeah, one guard would still have the gun and the cattle prod. But Michael had the power to pick a vein, any vein, in the guard's head, then give the lucky winner vein a good squeeze. It would be lights-out for the guard. Uh-huh.

But there were two guards, and both had their eyes locked on him. It's like they didn't even allow themselves to blink at the same time. But if Michael didn't make any sudden moves or anything, for, say, six months or a year, they might start to slack off.

Michael stifled a groan as he flopped back on the bed. Man, there wasn't even a TV in here or anything. The only entertainment he had was a whole bunch of empty cells exactly like his. And the guards.

He sat back up and scanned the floor. Weren't prison cells supposed to come with a mouse or a spider? Something for the prisoner to slowly make friends with? My inmate rights are definitely being violated here, he thought. Call the warden.

At least Max and Isabel were okay. He could focus on that. A while ago, he wasn't sure how long—it was tough keeping track of time in this windowless hellhole—he'd felt a burst of overwhelming joy and relief from Isabel. That meant Isabel got out of the compound safely. And hopefully, that Max made the connection to the collective consciousness and lived.

Michael heard a soft clicking sound and jerked his head toward the glass door just as Guard Number One swung it open.

"You're wanted in the lab," the guard announced, his voice flat and expressionless.

The lab. The words liquefied Michael's guts. He didn't know exactly what happened to a suspected alien in *the lab*. But it didn't sound promising. He shoved himself to his feet. Even his bones felt soft

14

and soggy, but he was determined not to let Bachelor Number One and Bachelor Number Two know that he was seriously freaking out. He swaggered over to the door nonchalantly.

The guards made a Michael sandwich—one in front of him, one in back—and marched him across the huge warehouse of a room that contained the cells. The first guard punched a code into the little box next to a massive metal door, careful not to let Michael see the numbers. The doors slid open down the middle, and they walked down a long corridor, their feet pounding out a rhythm on the cement floor.

"You guys know any of those marching chants?" Michael asked to distract himself. "You know, like, 'I don't know, but it's been said, yadda, yadda, yadda.' 'Cause that's what we need right now."

Neither Hubba nor Bubba bothered to answer him. Big surprise.

I don't know, but it's been said, compound guards all wet their bed. The words just popped into his mind, and he gave a snort of laughter. Alex is rubbing off on me, Michael thought. The more tense a situation got, the more stupid Alex's jokes became.

At least the chant kept him from screaming or puking. Still, his heart was practically ricocheting off his ribs with every beat.

I don't know, but I've been told, compound

15

guards all . . . hmmm . . . all have breath that smells like mold?

The first guard stopped in front of another metal door and punched in the code. It slid open and the odor of antiseptic, powder, plastic, and something unidentifiable, something chemical, filled Michael's nose. Lab smell. The guards escorted Michael inside. There was a padded examination table in the far corner and a metal tray of instruments on the counter behind it.

Hot bile rose up the back of his throat, and for one moment he was afraid he was going to do the Technicolor yawn right there. He swallowed hard.

"Oh, good. Our guest of honor has arrived." Michael turned toward the door, knowing he would see Sheriff Valenti. He met the sheriff's gaze and held it, willing himself not to blink.

"Should we get started?" a voice Michael didn't recognize asked. The question ended his staring contest with the sheriff. They both turned toward the man in the white lab coat.

"Yes, there's a lot I want to cover this session," Valenti answered.

"Okay, go have a seat at that table," the doctor told Michael.

At least it wasn't the padded examination table. It was just your basic cafeteria kind of table with a bench on either side. Michael walked over and sat down. Valenti slid onto the bench across from him.

Out of his peripheral vision he caught the doctor's hand moving in, and a second later Michael felt something cold and gooey on his forehead. He jerked back his head and found himself staring directly into the doctor's face.

Michael started, then laughed out loud at himself. Man, I am jittery, he thought.

"I'm glad my face amuses you," the doctor said. "I'm Dr. Doyle. Brian Doyle. I should have said that up front."

"Can we get on with it?" Valenti demanded.

The lab rat doesn't need to know names, right, Sheriff? Michael thought.

Dr. Doyle stuck a tiny plastic suction cup over the gel he'd applied. Michael could see a wire running from the cup to a monitor. He wasn't a science head like Max or Liz, but he knew they were going to look at his brain waves. At least he was pretty sure that was the deal.

But who knows what kind of technology these Project Clean Slate guys have? he thought as the doctor attached more suction cups to his head. Maybe the doc and the sheriff are about to fry my brain to make sure I'm being a good little prisoner who would never think of causing any problem—because I can no longer think at all. Sort of like a lobotomy without the mess.

"Done," Dr. Doyle announced. He sat down next to Michael.

"All right, the first thing I want you to show us is how you made yourself look like me," Valenti instructed. "I was told that's how you were able to enter the compound undetected."

I'm not that easy, Michael thought. The less the sheriff knew about him and his powers, the better.

"Here's how it worked. I stopped by the costume shop on North Main and picked up a latex mask. I got the last one of you. The counter guy told me you're one of the most popular Halloween costumes this year. You beat out Frankenstein and most of the cast of *Star Trek* and—"

"Enough," Valenti snapped. He turned to the guards at the door. "One of you go get Adam." Immediately one of the guards hurried out of the room.

"I'm not sure that's such a good idea," Dr. Doyle said quickly. "We don't know how two—"

"The kid doesn't want to talk. He wants to be a comedian," Valenti interrupted. "So I'll get the info another way."

Michael gathered that he was supposed to be scared of this Adam guy. Who was he? Some kind of torture expert or something?

The big metal door slid open with a soft hiss, and a guy who looked a little younger than Michael entered, followed by the guard.

This was Adam? This was the guy Valenti was hoping could get the truth out of Michael? He looked more like the kind of guy who'd always gotten his lunch money stolen—almost no muscles, I-spend-my-days-hunched-over-a-computer pale, light brown hair cut into dorky bangs, and wide pale green eyes. The kind of guy that might make certain girls go *aww*, but not much of an intimidator.

Michael shot a glance at Valenti. What was going on here?

"Hello, Adam." Valenti smiled at the kid. "We have a visitor with us today. His name is Michael. I want you to play the game with Michael," Valenti continued.

Adam hurried over to Michael, and before Michael had a chance to react, Adam grabbed his hand. Instantly they were connected. A rush of images flashed through Michael's brain. A younger Dr. Doyle sliding a little boy Adam into a big hollow tube for a CAT scan. A slightly older Adam in a glass cell playing checkers with a uniformed guard. A tray with silver instruments. A vial of blood. A pair of cowboy pajamas. An incubation pod. Adam breaking free of an incubation pod.

Michael jerked his hand away and stared at Adam. He was one of them. No question. Hadn't Ray said there was one pod he hadn't been able to move to the cave? It must have been Adam's.

And the Project Clean Slate agents recovered it.

"Michael, what did you see when Adam touched you?" Dr. Doyle asked. He pulled a little pad and a pen out of his lab coat pocket.

"Holding hands with another guy doesn't exactly make me see fireworks, if that's what you mean," Michael muttered.

He was still trying to take this all in. Had Adam spent his whole life here in the compound? Had they actually made a little kid spend year after year underground?

"Adam, what did you see?" Valenti asked, in a demented preschool teacher voice.

All Michael had been thinking about was the images he got from Adam. But if Adam was one of them, that meant he had power, too. So during the connection, Adam had been getting a little peek into Michael's brain.

"I saw a man in a surgical mask," Adam answered, his voice quiet and steady. "I saw a map of the desert. I saw him breaking out of a metal cocoon like mine," Adam continued.

He saw the pod. Now they know for sure I'm an alien, Michael thought. But it's not like there was a whole lot of doubt about that. They didn't exactly buy the Valenti Halloween mask story.

"Anything else?" Valenti asked gently.

"A girl. With long blond hair and blue eyes," Adam said.

"Tell us more about her," Valenti coaxed.

Of course, Michael thought, this game's purpose is to find the other aliens in Roswell.

"She was wearing a short skirt—green and black," Adam answered.

Isabel, Michael thought. Isabel in her cheerleading outfit. Thank God he hadn't picked up her name . . . yet.

Isabel smoothed down her short green-and-black skirt. The next time she was going to get it right. On the "*bray*" of *celebration* she was supposed to lean down so on the "*tion*" Stacey Scheinin could jump on her back for the big end-of-cheer pose. Isabel could do that. She'd done it a hundred times before. Although none of those hundred times had been today. Today she was biting the big one.

Yeah, and there's no reason for it, right? Isabel asked herself. Just because your brother almost died yesterday. Oh, and because Michael is locked up in the compound.

At least Isabel knew Michael was alive. She could feel his fear and anger so strongly, it was almost like he was standing next to her, whispering in her ear. Most of the time she just tuned out the emotions she got from Max and Michael, but now she wished she could feel them as powerfully as he was feeling them himself. She wanted to know everything Michael was going through. "Okay, I know that you all have places to go," Stacey cried in her squeaky, I-suck-helium voice. "But no one's leaving until we get this perfect. Are you listening, Isabel? I know you're dying to get over to your *boyfriend*. I guess that's what you'd call him." Stacey shot a look over at Alex, who was sitting in the bleachers. "Even though he hardly deserves that title."

About half the girls broke into loud giggles, the girls Isabel called the Staceyettes. Their biggest ambition in life was to be just like Stacey, and that meant laughing at all the little jabs Stacey made at Isabel.

The girl was loving the fact that Isabel was going out with Alex. Not that Alex was a geek. But before Alex, Isabel had gone out strictly with guys in the elite club, the guys that every girl in school wanted, the totally obvious choices. Alex was cute and smart, but not an *obvious* Isabel choice.

Tish Okabe leaned close. "Are you okay?" she whispered. That was Tish. Always worrying about how everyone else was feeling.

"Uh-huh. Fine," Isabel answered. Instantly she felt a sharp burst of fear. It was coming from Michael. She concentrated on her feelings for him and tried to shoot him back a burst of . . . of love. That's what it was. She'd always loved Michael. First as sort of a second big brother, someone who made her feel safe. Then as a teenage crush. Then as . . . what? As a friend? More than that. A brother? That didn't feel quite—

"You're fine," Tish said softly, pulling Isabel away from her thoughts. "That's why you're letting Stacey dis your man without counterdissing."

Oh. Yeah. She probably should slap Stacey down. Isabel had been letting her get away with way too much lately. "Yeah, it's true. Alex is nothing like your boyfriends," Isabel called to Stacey. "When he walks, his knuckles don't quite drag the ground."

Not her best comeback, but she felt lucky she managed to get anything out at all. Only a weensy bit of her brain was on Stacey or practice or Alex. The rest was on Michael.

"Ready, okay!" Stacey called. And Isabel launched into the cheer. For the next two minutes she needed to focus on getting her arms and legs in the right position and keeping her cheerleader smile on her face because she really, really did not want to have to do this cheer again.

Okay, you're doing fine. Just keep your head up, she coached herself. Smile. Now the shoulder shimmy. Pivot left. Pivot right. Smile, smile, smile. Halfway through. You're doing good. Now Tish does her walkover. Now Corrine. Now you. Perfect. Keep going. Okay, now move into position for the final pose. Bend down.

A bolt of ragged-edged anger and hatred jabbed into Isabel. She stumbled just as Stacey jumped onto her back—and Stacey landed on her butt with a squeal. She shoved herself to her feet, her face pink with anger. "Okay, let's do it again. Right away," Stacey announced. "We'll see if Isabel can do this without injuring me."

This must be what hell is like, Isabel thought. Having to do the same cheer over and over and over, smiling and smiling, knowing the whole time that someone you love is suffering.

"I have to be at work in fifteen minutes," Lucinda Baker told Stacey. "And my boss definitely won't accept a note from my head cheerleader as an excuse."

"I have to go, too," Tish chimed in.

Thank you, Isabel thought. She took a moment to focus on shooting Michael another burst of emotion. She'd never consciously tried to send Max or Michael emotions before this. She hoped it was working. She wanted Michael to feel like she was right there in the compound with him.

"Fine. Go," Stacey cried. "But be back here at seven tomorrow morning. We're not going to the Guffman game without having this cheer down," she continued, her voice getting higher and higher until Isabel thought dogs were probably starting to howl all over town.

Isabel spun around and rushed toward the locker room. "I just have to change," she told Alex as she started past the bleachers.

He reached out and snagged her hand. "I don't want you to change."

Isabel tried to pull her hand away, but he held tight. "I know, I know, you're going to tell me you like me just the way I am," she said.

"Nope. Although I do like you pretty much the way you are," he added quickly. "I don't want you to change because I've never gotten to kiss you while you're wearing the uniform." He pulled her closer until she was standing between his knees.

"Oh, it turns you on, huh?" she asked. She wanted to look over her shoulder and see if Stacey was watching, but Isabel didn't want to give her the satisfaction.

"Big time," he answered. He slid his hand up her leg. "Especially the green underpants. Or are they underpants? I mean, do you wear other underpants under them or what?" He slid his hand higher, slipping it under her skirt.

"Some things just have to remain a mystery." Isabel slapped Alex's hand away, and he laughed.

"Okay, okay, you're right. It would be like knowing how a magician really gets the rabbit out of his hat. It's more fun not knowing." Alex pulled her down on the bleacher next to him.

Oh, who cares if Stacey *is* watching, Isabel thought. As soon as she started kissing Alex she'd forget all about her. That was one of the best things about kissing him. It's like the kiss was a minivacation from the world. She could really use that right now.

Alex laced his hands through her hair, then brushed his mouth across hers. Sweet. Sometimes Alex's kisses could just be so sweet.

He slid his hands slowly down her back, then kissed her again, his tongue urging her lips apart. *What emotion is Michael getting from me right now?* Isabel thought suddenly. *Can he tell I'm having some big make-out session while he's—*

Alex pulled away. "Are you all right?"

"Yeah. Yeah."

Isabel nodded, then she stood up. "I'll be right back," she said, then she headed toward the locker room. *That's the first time kissing Alex didn't make the rest of the world disappear,* she thought.

Liar, a tiny voice in the back of her head answered. *Kissing Alex hasn't been like that since you went into Michael's dream and saw him with his arms around you.*

"I wish I was a . . . you know," Maria told Liz. She snapped an order on the metal wheel and gave it a spin toward the kitchen. "They don't want cheese on that Mother Ship Burger," she called to Stan, the cook.

"Actually, I don't know," Liz answered. "A what?"

"A *you know,*" Maria repeated. She glanced around the Crashdown Café. There were only a few customers at the flying-saucer-shaped tables, and no one seemed to be paying any attention to her

28

and Liz. But Maria still didn't think it was a good idea to use the *a* word.

Liz shook her head. "Can you act it out for me or something? Because I have no idea what you're talking about."

"A you know, like, you know, Isabel and Max and Michael," Maria whispered.

"Really?" Liz adjusted the scrunchie holding her long, dark hair away from her face. "Even after everything that's happened? Earth hasn't exactly been the friendliest place for them."

"It's just that Isabel and Max can *feel* Michael all the time," Maria explained. "They know a little bit of what he's going through. They know . . ." She hesitated. It felt almost like it would be bad luck to finish the sentence. "They can feel inside them . . . that Michael's still alive."

Maria was going psycho with worry. Michael was all she could think about. What was happening to him in the compound? What was Valenti doing to him?

It's not like Isabel would have the answers to those questions. But at least she'd know if Michael was experiencing pain, if he was scared or angry. At least Isabel still had *some* connection to Michael. Maria had nothing. Just an aching empty place inside her chest that felt like it got bigger with every second Michael was away from her.

"He's not going to die. Think about it. He's way

too valuable to Sheriff Valenti alive. For one thing, Michael has information Valenti wants. He would never kill him until he found the other . . . *you knows*." Liz took a deep breath, then continued. "And we're going to get him out of there before that happens."

Maria nodded. "I know. I know. I still just wish—"

The opening bars of the *Close Encounters* theme interrupted her. She glanced toward the door to see who was coming in. Alex. Good. Maybe Alex could get them onto another subject.

"So, what do you think of months-of-the-year underpants?" Alex asked as he slid onto one of the stools lining the counter.

"What?" Liz cried.

"I'm making a list of very bad business ideas for my web site," Alex explained.

"Who changes their underwear every month?" Maria asked. "Now if they made some that just had the year on them, those would sell like crazy." She held on to her straight face for half a second, then started to giggle.

"Is she mocking me?" Alex asked Liz. "I think she's mocking me."

Maria kept giggling. She couldn't stop. She giggled so hard, her stomach started to hurt and tears stung her eyes. She wanted to stop. But she couldn't.

Liz shoved a glass of water into her hand, and

Maria took a swallow. It went down the wrong way and she started to choke, her nose and throat and lungs burning as she coughed and sputtered.

Alex leaned across the counter and pounded her on the back. Maria gave one more cough and managed to pull in a breath. She grabbed a napkin out of the dispenser and wiped her eyes and then her running nose.

"Are you okay?" Liz asked.

"Yeah. Just totally embarrassed," Maria answered. She folded the napkin and wiped her eyes again. The tears wouldn't stop streaming. God, she really was going psycho. She took a quick glance around the café. "Everyone is staring at me."

"Order up," Stan called from the kitchen.

"I'll get it," Liz told Maria. She grabbed the plates and hurried into the dining room.

"You sure you're okay?" Alex asked. He pulled another napkin out of the dispenser and handed it to her.

"Yeah," Maria answered. "So, um, why are you here?" she asked, trying to sound sane. "I mean, I thought you and Isabel were going to the mall after she got done with practice."

"She wasn't in the mood," Alex said, obviously frustrated. "She also wasn't in the mood to come here. Or in the mood for me to hang out at her house," he added.

"You're not thinking it has anything to do with

you, right?" Maria asked. "I'm sure she just needed some time by herself. She's totally freaked about Michael."

"Yeah," Alex agreed. "It's just that . . ."

"It's just that what?" she asked.

"It's just that even before Michael was captured, I had the feeling she was, I don't know . . . ," Alex said. "Take that party we went to last week. Isabel disappeared on me for, like, an hour."

"Wow, a whole hour?" Maria teased gently. But her stomach was curling up in a little ball. She knew where Isabel had been. She had been out in the backyard, standing very close to Michael.

Was Isabel the reason Michael hadn't said anything—well, much of anything—when Maria had told him she loved him?

Michael's eyes snapped open when he heard the door of his cell open. What now?

"We thought you two might want to play cards or something," one of the guards said. He stood back and let Adam walk into the cell, then locked the door behind him.

Do I look like a complete moron? Michael thought. Do they think that I don't know why they're doing this? They're looking for information. They're hoping I'll let something slip that will help them track down the others. Or that their little tame alien will make another connection with me and get better stuff than he did the last time.

Yeah, Adam saw Isabel when he made the connection in the lab. But he didn't see anything that indicated she was anything but a hot human chick that Michael had an image of in his brain. So Isabel should be safe for now. But Michael needed to be on guard around Adam. As much as he looked like a harmless kid—Michael had to keep reminding himself they were around the same age—Adam could be very dangerous.

Michael shot a glance at him. Adam was standing with his back practically pressed against the cell door. He looked like he wished he was anywhere but here. *I wonder what they told him about me?* Michael thought. *I wonder what they told him about* himself*? Does he even know he's from another planet? Or does he just think that everyone hatches out of a metal cocoon and grows up in little glass cells?*

"You want to play cards?" Michael asked, trying to sound reassuring without slipping into that Mr. Rogers–speak Valenti used with Adam. "Come on, we'll play." He slid down to the end of the bed so Adam had some room. Adam hesitated, then he walked over and sat down across from Michael.

"You know that game we played in the lab?" Michael asked. Adam immediately reached for Michael's hand to make the connection, and Michael jerked away. "I don't like that game. Don't ever try to play that game with me unless I say it's okay. You understand?" he asked.

Adam nodded, his green eyes wary. "Good," Michael said. "So what game do you want to play?"

"Crazy eights is my favorite," Adam answered. He pulled a deck of cards out of his pocket and started to deal.

Crazy eights. Man. Michael tried to remember the last time he'd played that game. A while ago. He wasn't even sure he still remembered the rules.

"Cool," Michael told him. "That's my favorite game, too." He felt a little slimy saying it, but he needed Adam to start trusting him. Michael had already decided that when he found a way out of here, Adam was coming with him. There was no way Michael was leaving one of his own in this pit.

Adam flipped over the top card in the pile that sat between him and Michael—a three of hearts. Then he picked up his own cards, studied them quickly, and slapped down the jack of hearts.

Oh, right, Michael thought. You just have to match suits. Or you can match the numbers if you want. It was all coming back to him. He grabbed his cards, found a heart, and put it on top of Adam's. Adam slammed down the two of hearts. Michael started to put down the two of clubs.

"No! You have to take two. Take two! When I play a two, you have to take two!" Adam pointed to the two of hearts on the pile and gave a joyful cackle.

Michael couldn't stop himself from smiling as he took his two cards. Adam was really getting into the game. It reminded Michael of Isabel as a little girl. She'd always played Candy Land as if she had a million bucks riding on the game. She cheated, too. She'd trick you into looking out the window or at the TV, then she'd plant the card she needed at the top of the pile.

But Izzy was seven years old at the time. And

Adam had to be sixteen or seventeen. Michael felt hot anger begin to boil inside him. Adam was one of them, which meant he could absorb information much faster than humans did. If someone gave him some books or a computer, he'd soak up knowledge by the second. Instead he was still getting all hyped over a game of crazy eights.

"So who taught you how to play this game?" Michael asked. He didn't plan on giving Adam any info, but that didn't mean he wasn't going to try and get some.

"Dad," Adam answered. He snapped down the two of diamonds and laughed when Michael had to add two more cards to his hand.

"And who would that be?" Michael asked.

"Mr. Valenti," Adam returned.

Dad? Adam called the man who kept him prisoner underground *Dad*. And Michael thought he'd had it bad doing the foster-home boogie all his life. There were worse things, much worse things.

"Did, uh, *Dad*"—the name tasted like acid on Michael's tongue—"teach you how to play the other game, too?"

"Uh-uh. I always knew how to play it," Adam answered as he added another card to the pile.

"And what about . . . Daddy Valenti. Can he play it, too?" Michael thought it was a good idea to get Adam thinking about the way he and Valenti were different. Because at some point—some point soon—Michael was going to have to tell Adam the truth about the sheriff. It would be a lot easier to get Adam out of here if he actually wanted to leave, and Michael didn't think that would happen until Adam knew that the sheriff didn't deserve one scrap of loyalty . . . or love. How twisted was it that Valenti had manipulated Adam into loving him? Because Adam did. Michael could hear it in Adam's voice when he said Valenti's name.

Adam laughed. "No. It's not a game for daddies," he answered, in an everybody-knows-that tone.

Duh. Michael should have known Valenti would have come up with a reason why he could never play the game with Adam. The images that Adam would get from Valenti would make it very clear that Dad was, well, not a very nice guy.

"It's your turn," Adam reminded him.

"Oh, right. Now let me see." Michael pulled one card out of his hand, then replaced it. He bit his lip in an exaggerated way as he selected another card, then put it back.

Adam laughed like this was the funniest thing he'd ever seen. This guy had to get out more.

Michael added a card to the pile, then he caught a flash of movement off to his right. He glanced over and saw Valenti and two guards walking a girl down the row of cells. "Who's she?" he asked Adam.

Adam turned, and his mouth dropped open a little. "I don't know," he whispered.

He sounded kind of awestruck. Judging by Adam's behavior, Michael thought it was probably the first female that Adam had ever seen—at least, the first one close to his age. Adam had some great surprises waiting for him if they ever managed to make it aboveground.

Although the girl who had just walked in would stand out even up there, where there was a lot more competition. She was tall and lean, with red hair that was even shorter than his. But the hair didn't make her look at all boyish.

What could she possibly be doing down here? Whatever it was, she didn't look pleased about it. One of the guards pulled open the door of the cell across from Michael's and thrust the girl inside with a rough push. The girl didn't turn around. She just stood there, her back straight, her head up, refusing to look at any of them.

Michael wouldn't wish for anyone to be pushed into that stuffy cell. But if someone had to be there, he was glad it was someone who looked like her.

Cameron Winger kept her back turned so she didn't have to see the door close behind her, locking her inside the glass cell. She wished the sheriff had told her more about what was going to happen to her. Tests, that's all he said. A series of tests beginning tomorrow. Tests. That could mean almost anything. It could mean sitting at a desk, filling in a million of those little bubbles. Or it could mean—Cameron didn't want to think about what else it could mean. It was pointless. Because whatever it meant, she would have to go through with it. The sheriff would see to that.

Cameron was good at evaluating people, and she'd already figured out Sheriff Valenti wasn't a guy who could be made to feel pity. Or much of anything else. She doubted he could squeeze out an emotion if his life depended on it, and that meant once he decided to do something, he did it. If Cameron changed her mind about the tests, she had the feeling she could cry an ocean of tears, then scream her lungs out, then throw a total kicking, screaming, mouth-foaming fit without Valenti even raising an eyebrow. Or getting close to letting her go.

Cameron spun around and found the two guards and the sheriff staring at her. She had the wild impulse to shove her face against the glass and make fish faces at them. That's exactly what her cell was like—a big aquarium. Except instead of a fish, she was more like one of those lobsters in a restaurant tank, the ones with their claws taped closed who were only a big boiling pot of water away from being dinner.

She returned the sheriff's gaze steadily, trying not to feel like a lobster. He finally turned and strode away.

Cameron wondered what the two guys in the cell across from hers had done to get themselves in here. The one with the silky light brown hair looked like he should still be getting tucked in by Mom, even though she figured he was around her age.

The other guy, the one with the spiked hair, now, he looked dangerous. In all kinds of ways. He had gray eyes like the sheriff's. But this guy's eyes were burning with emotion. He looked like the tortured soul type, which, unfortunately, she had always been attracted to.

She formed her hand into a lobster claw and clicked it at him. The lopsided grin that broke across his face made her feel alive—for the moment.

Max took a deep breath, then turned the key and swung open the door to Ray's apartment. He caught a whiff of something that smelled like baking powder. He knew the scent was part of a message from the collective consciousness, so he ignored it. He had been trying to talk to Ray through the consciousness, but he couldn't figure out how. All he'd gotten was a wave of images, odors, sounds, and sensations, all with pieces of information attached to them. Usually Max would have loved learning so much about his home planet and his people. But it was harder to get excited with Ray . . . gone. And Michael captured.

Max stepped into the apartment and shut the door behind him. He headed down the hall to Ray's bedroom. A smile tugged at his lips as he passed the living room with the beanbag chairs that were Ray's version of wall-to-wall carpeting. Ray was such a goofball.

A hard lump formed in Max's throat at the thought. It was so hard to accept that he'd never hear Ray's corny jokes again. Or see his Elvis impersonation. And Max was still trying to deal with the fact that no matter how bad things got, Ray would never be able to come to the rescue. "I'm going to miss you," he whispered. "And not just because you kept saving our butts."

This isn't the time for a touching soap-opera moment, he told himself. He needed to do a sweep of the apartment to make sure there wasn't anything lying around that, say, offered incontrovertible proof of the existence of life on other planets. Max stepped into Ray's bedroom. The first thing he saw was Ray's I Survived the Roswell Incident T-shirt lying on the bed. He snorted. That wasn't exactly proof. Half the people in town had that shirt.

Max picked up the shirt and pulled it over the T-shirt he was wearing. He wanted something of Ray's to keep, something to remember him by. And the shirt—it was so Ray. He wasn't going to find anything better, plus he was pretty sure Ray would like the idea of passing the shirt on to another true Roswell Incident survivor.

He turned and slid open the mirrored closet door. There were a bunch more T-shirts, some jeans, some chinos, three pairs of sneakers, and one of the spangled Elvis jumpsuits Ray had them wear at the museum when he first put up the display showing the connection between the King and aliens. That was it. Ray hadn't exactly been going for the best-dressed award.

Max moved on to the dresser. He shook the big peanut butter jar full of pennies, then tapped all four of the little guitar-playing aliens so that their heads bobbed. He quickly checked the three big drawers. Nothing but some underwear, some bolo ties, and a big stuffed gorilla holding a tiny Empire State Building. Okay.

He took one last glance around the bedroom and hurried down to the bathroom. Toothpaste and bath oil. Okay again.

Now all he had to do was check the kitchen and he was out of there. He was glad, too. The search was starting to feel creepy.

Max hurried to the kitchen and pulled open the closest cabinet door. Way too many boxes of that cereal with the marshmallow rockets. Max guessed Ray didn't have any problem starting the day with a lot of artificial colors and sugar.

He opened the next cabinet, and he felt a

pricking sensation across the back of his neck. Dingdong, collective consciousness calling, he thought. Wasn't there some way of putting a Do Not Disturb sign in his brain? He didn't have time to deal with that stuff right now.

Max heard the click of boot heels coming down the hall, and he realized that the neck prickling wasn't coming from the collective consciousness. It was a response to the fact that he wasn't alone in the apartment.

He swung around. Sheriff Valenti stood there, his eyes hidden by his mirrored sunglasses.

"Oh my God!" Max blurted out. "You scared me."

Valenti smiled.

"I guess you want to know what I'm doing here." Great start, Max, he thought.

Valenti nodded.

"I wanted to check on my boss, Ray Iburg," Max said. "This is his place. When I showed up for work today, the museum wasn't open. So I came up here. Ray gave me a key a while ago."

"Any idea where he is?" Valenti asked. "The museum was closed yesterday, too. I became concerned."

Maybe you should have been concerned *before* you shot him, Max thought. What was the sheriff's game? Was he trying to figure out if Max knew the truth about Ray? Or had Valenti tortured Michael into telling him that Max and Isabel were the two remaining aliens Valenti had been searching for all these years? Max was getting no clue from Valenti's expressionless face.

"He didn't say he was going out of town or anything," Max answered. His scalp felt all itchy. He wanted to scratch it, but he thought he'd look too nervous. He used both hands to shove his blond hair off his face instead.

"Uh-huh," Valenti answered. "Well, when Mr. Iburg does return, please tell him to check in with me. And if you hear anything, call." He turned and strode out of the kitchen, obviously expecting Max to follow.

He knows more than he's saying, Max thought as he trailed Valenti down the hall. But how much more?

"All right," Dr. Doyle said. "Now I want you to link to Bill and see if you can tell me what his mother looks like."

"Do I get a piece of cheese if I do?" Michael muttered. Adam seemed perfectly happy to do anything the doctor asked. He seemed to believe all the tests were games, just like crazy eights. And why wouldn't he? This was his only reality.

"Are you tired? Do you need a break?" Doyle asked Michael.

"No. Let the games begin," Michael answered.

Michael reached out and touched the arm of Bill, the lucky test subject. He took a few deep breaths as he tried to make the connection. Come on, Bill. Give it up, he thought. Yeah, there. He had it. The images were starting to flow. A spilled glass of orange juice on a tile floor. A geeky teenage Bill trying to pin a corsage on a girl's strapless dress. A casket being lowered into the ground. Yoda.

The images kept speeding by Michael. He'd never tried to pull a specific memory out of anyone's head before, which was what Dr. Doyle wanted him to do. Michael concentrated all his attention on one of the images as it sped by and managed to freeze it.

It was a car. A Plymouth Barracuda. As he studied it, some information came to him. He just *knew* that the car belonged to Bill's grandmother. He called her Honey because she thought being called Grandma made her sound too old. Honey and Bill had made a trip to Vegas in the Barracuda when Bill was ten and a half. She snuck him into one of the casinos and he won five bucks on a nickel slot machine.

Very nice. Touching. But Michael was supposed to find out what Bill's mother looked like. He released his hold on the image of the car, and the images started streaking by him again. A cat with a torn ear. Sheriff Valenti. An airline flight attendant.

Come on, Mom. Where are you? Michael thought. Then he felt his hand being pulled off Bill's arm. The connection broke.

"Were you able to get a picture of his mother?" Dr. Doyle asked.

Michael shook his head. "I don't control what I see," he answered. He wouldn't mind playing around with this on his own to figure out if there was a way to pull out specific information during a connection, but he wasn't all that eager to give the Project Clean Slate guys any helpful hints about acquiring this technology. If he did, Big Brother wouldn't be satisfied with just watching. Big Brother would start opening up people's heads and poking around with a stick.

Dr. Doyle made a note on his little pad. "Adam hasn't been able to select the information he receives, either," he said. "I'd like to try the same test again. Except this time I'd like you and Adam to link to each other and then link to Bill."

Adam shot Michael a questioning look. Michael nodded his permission. He didn't want Adam to connect to him again, but he didn't think there was a way around it. If he refused, Daddy Valenti could just strap him to a table and then have Adam connect.

When Adam touched Michael's wrist, the connection was instantaneous, effortless. As soon as the images from Adam started, Michael grabbed Bill's arm, and the images from Bill replaced the ones from Adam.

Okay, we're looking for Bill's mother here, Michael thought. The images from Bill sped by faster and faster until they were a blur of color. Michael couldn't make out anything at all. Then—bam!—one image exploded in front of him, filling his entire field of vision. Hello, Mom.

Information about her started pouring into him. Dr. Doyle broke the connection before he could absorb even a fraction of it.

"She smelled like lemons," Adam announced.

Dr. Doyle shot a look at Bill. "Yeah. She liked this lemon shampoo," Bill confirmed.

Michael felt energized and alert. He had connected with Max and Isabel many times and even used his power at the same time they'd used theirs. But he'd never connected with one of them and then used their *combined* power. Who knew what they'd be able to do?

"Let's try it again. This time I want you to see if you can get the code to open the door to this lab. Of course, if you do, we'll have to change it." Dr. Doyle gave a little laugh.

You should have your own HBO special, Michael thought. You're a regular laugh riot.

Just as Adam reached for his wrist, the lab door swung open. Sheriff Valenti entered, followed by the girl from the cell across from Michael's. "This is Cameron Winger, the one I told you about," Valenti informed the doctor. "I'm interested in how her parapsychological powers can be used in conjunction with their abilities." He jerked his chin toward Michael and Adam. "I assume you've devised the appropriate tests."

Parapsychological powers. Was that like ESP or what? Michael thought.

"Of course," Doyle answered quickly. "Come over here and sit between Michael and Adam."

"What's their deal?" she asked, glancing at them.

"There's no need for you to speak unless you're asked a direct question," Valenti answered.

"Fine. I'll just squeak once for yes and twice for no. How's that?" Cameron sauntered over and slid into the chair next to Michael. She glanced over at him. "What was your name again? Mickey?"

"Uh-huh. And you're Minnie, right?" he asked.

"No. The Brain. World domination meeting at midnight. My cell," she whispered, leaning a little closer.

He caught the scent of something familiar. What was it? He knew he'd smelled it before. The beach, he realized. She smells exactly like the beach. Michael had only been to the beach once in his life. The Evanses took him there on vacation once. The best week of his life. He pulled in a deep breath, trying not to be too obvious about it. Oh, yeah.

"I need to ask you not to talk to each other," Dr. Doyle told them, with an anxious look at Valenti. "I'm going to have you do some telepathy drills, and it will taint the results if you know anything about each other."

"I'll expect a full report on my desk by the end of the day," Valenti told the doctor. He turned and started toward the door.

"Dad!" Adam called out to Valenti excitedly. "Michael and I made a link, then linked to Bill. It only took us two seconds to see his mother."

"That's very good," Valenti answered in his Mr. Rogers voice.

"Yes, very good, Igor," Michael mocked.

"Watch yourself, Michael. We do have punishments for attitude problems, you know," Valenti snapped back. He stared at Michael for a moment, then walked away, pulling the doctor with him.

As he whispered orders to the doctor, Michael's anger took hold of him. The "dad" stuff was just too much. Watching Adam's boyish face as he looked admiringly at that evil man. Michael couldn't deal with it anymore; Adam had to know the truth about Daddy Valenti. What if, he thought, Adam connected to . . . ah, yes.

"Adam," he said impishly. "Go play the game with Daddy Valenti. I know it's not really for daddies, but I bet he'll think it's really cool."

A wide smile broke across Adam's face. He leaped up and hurled himself at Valenti. Before Valenti could react, Adam grabbed his hand.

Michael knew the second Adam made the connection. He let out a high, keening wail that Michael could feel in the center of his bones.

"If Michael had told Valenti the truth about you and Isabel, neither of you would be sitting here right now," Alex said. He glanced around the Evanses' living room. Liz, Maria, Max, and Isabel all seemed to agree.

His gaze lingered on Isabel. Why was she sitting in the armchair? The minute they'd walked in the room, she practically ran toward it. It's not like he had to be within touching distance of her every moment of the day, though he wouldn't complain. But she didn't have to avoid him.

Oh, man. What did I tell you about hanging out with Liz and Maria so much? he asked himself. You're suffering from an attack of girl brain. Guys don't analyze garbage like this. If you don't watch yourself, you're going to start actually wanting to see movies with Meg Ryan in them, and then—

"I don't know why we're even talking about this," Isabel said, pulling Alex out of his thoughts. "Michael would never give Valenti information about any of us."

"That's a little, uh, naive, don't you think?" Alex asked. "Valenti has ways of making people talk. I'm sure he could make me squeal like a pig and tell him everything he wanted to know."

"Yeah, but you're not Michael, are you?" Isabel asked.

Ooohhhh. That was harsh, even to a guy brain. Like Michael was just way more tough, or strong, or action-hero-like than Alex could ever dream of being.

Which maybe was true. But Isabel was supposed to be his girlfriend. Wasn't that supposed to mean that—

"So when are we going in after Michael?" Maria asked. Alex forced his attention back to the conversation. "It's been three days already."

"I don't think three days is long enough," Liz said gently.

"After the stone incident, they're going to be well prepared for escape attempts," Max added.

"Yeah, I think it's too soon," Alex agreed.

"You think," Isabel said. "That's all we've been hearing is what you think. What about what the rest of us think?"

It's temporary insanity, Alex told himself. Michael's practically like her brother. Cut her some slack. "Max, Liz, and Maria just said what they thought," Alex answered, trying to keep his tone neutral. "What about you? What do you think we should do?"

Isabel hesitated. "I think we should wait," she finally mumbled.

Silence filled the room. Alex could hear the clock in the kitchen ticking.

"So we'll wait," Max said at last. "We should all just be thinking of ways to get into the compound so that we'll be ready when we can do it."

Maria stood up. "I've got to get home. Mom's still in her postdivorce dating frenzy, and I want to make sure she doesn't raid my closet again."

"You want to do the bio homework together?" Liz asked Max.

"Sure," he answered, and they headed off down the hall toward his room.

Alex and Isabel were alone. Alex wished they'd

all stayed in the living room awhile. Which was the opposite of the way he usually felt.

Isabel didn't make any move to come over to the couch or even look in his direction. She has to be terrified, Alex thought. Not just of what's happening to Michael, but of what could happen to her.

He stood up and walked over to her chair. He sat down on the arm. Isabel didn't look at him. He reached out and smoothed a lock of hair off her forehead. "I know you're scared—"

Isabel jumped up, then spun around to face him. "You have no idea what I'm feeling," she cried.

"So tell me," he answered. He could hear the anger creeping into his voice, and he tried to clamp it down.

"Why should I?" she demanded. "Just because we've gone out a few times, that doesn't mean you have the right to know my every thought!"

"I don't think we need to be hearing this," Max said. He swung his bedroom door shut.

"Yeah," Liz agreed. Whatever was going on out there was between Alex and Isabel, and they definitely didn't need an audience.

She sat down on Max's bed and pulled her bio book out of her backpack. "I haven't read any of the chapter yet, have you?" she asked.

"No. I keep—"

"Thinking about Michael," Liz finished his sentence. "How do you think he's doing? I mean, what have you been feeling from him?"

"Anger. A lot of anger and frustration. But no pain. And not as much fear. I think they must be treating him okay," Max answered. "I can't stop picturing him down there, though. It makes me nuts. If anyone should be down there, it should be me. I'm the one who needed the crystals."

"Michael and Isabel are going to need them, too," Liz reminded him. "You just happened to go through your *akino* first."

"I know, I know. I keep telling myself that," Max answered.

"Well, start listening," Liz answered. She rooted around in her backpack until she found a rubber band. She tossed it to Max. "You should try this."

Max stared at it. "I don't get it."

"Put it around your wrist. Then every time you start thinking about how all this is your fault, you snap it, to sort of snap yourself out of it," Liz explained. "That's what my mom did when she wanted to stop smoking."

Max slid the rubber band over his wrist and then snapped the band. "That stings."

"It's supposed to," Liz said. "That's the point. It's supposed to jerk you out of your thought pattern or something. Although there *is* another method you could try." She tried to sound all serious, but she could feel her lips curving into a smile. "It's kind of experimental, though."

"It doesn't involve anything like placenta, does it?" Max asked. "It seems like every new cure has something to do with placenta. Did you see in the news about using blood from the placenta as sort of a substitute for a bone marrow transplant?"

"It has nothing to do with placenta," Liz promised. "It has to do with kissing me. See, whenever you're about to step on the plane for another one of your guilt trips, you kiss me instead."

"Well . . ." Max hesitated. "I guess I should keep an open mind about these new experimental treatments." He slid one hand under her hair, skimming his fingers over the sensitive skin of her neck. "I'm actually starting to feel a little guilty right now."

"Oh, really?" Liz wrapped her arms around his waist. "Well, let's see if the Ortecho method works." She kissed him—a long, slow kiss that spread warmth through her entire body. It was so amazing to be able to kiss Max whenever she wanted to. That was one good thing that came out of him getting so sick. He finally realized what a waste it was for them to be just friends.

Liz raised her head a fraction of an inch. "Did that help?" she asked, her lips still so close to Max's that they brushed against his with every word.

"Yeah. It did. A lot. But there's something else I'm feeling guilty about," Max answered. "I, um, um, I ate the last coconut cookie last night. And my dad loves coconut cookies. I just feel terrible about it," he said in a rush.

They kissed again. Liz's laughter turned into a little gasp as Max leaned back on the bed, pulling her down on top of him. Her long hair tumbled down, forming a curtain around their faces.

Liz felt like everyone in the entire world had vanished as Max began kissing her neck, flicking his tongue across the little hollow at the base of her throat. Every sense was filled with Max. Nothing else mattered.

Then she heard the front door slam.

Footsteps ran down the hall. And she thought she heard the sound of Isabel crying.

"Should we go out there and talk to her?" Liz asked.

"In a little while. She probably needs to be alone first." Max slid his hands down to Liz's waist. "Besides, I'm starting to feel sort of guilty again. It's not really fair that Isabel is fighting with her guy while I have you in my bedroom."

"Yeah," Liz breathed. "I'm feeling a little guilty about that, too."

Cameron strolled through the doorway of Michael's cell as if she couldn't even see the two guards with machine guns flanking it. "I'm having sort of a *Planet of the Apes* moment here," she said as they locked the door behind her. "You know that scene where they put the woman in the cage with Taylor the astronaut? Sort of as a present?"

Planet of the Apes, Michael thought. He and Maria had watched that during one of their late night movie marathons a few weeks ago. Back when things were normal between them, before she told him she loved him. He couldn't even think about that now. Not in here. It would make him stark-staring wacko.

"Yeah, I know the part you mean," Michael answered. He raised an eyebrow. "So am I supposed to unwrap you now?"

She snorted. "I wouldn't try it. Not unless you have a very high threshold of pain." She sat down on Michael's cot. "Where's your weird little friend?"

"Adam? The guards said they'd bring him over

later. The doctor wanted to do a couple more tests on him," Michael said.

"What's his story? Is he, you know, all there or what?" Cameron asked.

Michael felt a surge of protectiveness. He'd only known Adam a couple of days, but already he felt like family. The kid definitely needed someone to look after him, and since there wasn't exactly a line of volunteers for the job, Michael had decided to step in.

"Adam was born in this place," Michael explained. "Everyone here treats him like he's five years old, so that's the only way he knows to act."

Michael noticed Cameron's brown eyes widen a fraction. That got to her, he realized. She's not quite as hard as she thinks she is.

"And what about you, Mickey? What's your deal?" she asked.

"I just got here. The pictures the travel agent showed me made the accommodations look much more inviting," he said.

"It's true. The hot tubs were supposed to be pink marble. I don't know about yours, but mine is just white porcelain," she shot back, doing a snobby rich girl impersonation. "Unacceptable."

She ran one of her fingers back and forth along the rip in the knee of her jeans. Michael noticed she had a tattoo—some funky little design—on the back of her hand. Usually Michael thought tattoos were trendy and chintzy. But on Cameron it worked.

"No, really," she said. "How did you end up in here?"

Michael figured everyone in the compound knew he and Adam were aliens. But she obviously didn't. Yeah, there were some yellow splotches of fear in her olive green aura. But nothing like what he'd expect to see if she knew the truth. That was a whole different kind of fear than the fear of being held prisoner. It was the fear of the unknown. Of the *other*. Of the monster.

"You first," Michael answered. He didn't think it would be long before someone told Cameron the truth about him. But for now, for tonight, he didn't want to deal with her pulling away from him.

Cameron wrapped her arms around her knees and laced her long, graceful fingers together. "I ran away. Our friend the sheriff found me. He made this deal with my parents. If they'd allow me to live here and participate in some tests of my psychic abilities, he'd, I think the expression he used was, take me in hand. Meaning, make sure I studied enough to get good SAT scores. Make sure I didn't run away again. Basically make sure I was a good little girl."

"And they said yes?" Michael asked.

The edges of Cameron's aura darkened to an oily gray. "Oh, yeah. They said yes. I get the feeling he may have given them some cash to sweeten the deal." She let out her breath in a long sigh. "But even if he hadn't, they probably would have jumped on it. They aren't too crazy about having a freak for a daughter."

There are a lot of sick puppies in the world, Michael thought. People who would sell their own daughter . . . they had to be the sickest. "How old were you when you first realized you could . . . do things other people couldn't?"

Her aura's yellow splotches widened, the gray rim grew darker, and jagged streaks of red appeared. Talking about this was stressing her out majorly.

"You know what?" Michael said quickly. "It doesn't matter. We're both freaks. That's really all we need to know about each other. Let's talk about something else."

"Like getting out of here," Cameron agreed, her voice low and tense.

"Wait. They're bringing Adam over," Michael cautioned. He and Cameron watched in silence as two guards escorted Adam to the cell. Michael could hardly stand to look at Adam's face. The color was drained, and his eyes . . . his eyes looked dead. No more life in them than a couple of marbles.

"What did they do to him?" Cameron whispered.

"It's what I did to him," Michael answered.

"Remember when he touched the sheriff and started screaming? He was screaming because he saw images from the sheriff's brain. I don't know which ones exactly, but I know for sure he could have seen the sheriff kill a couple different people."

"Wait. How is that something you did?" Cameron asked.

"I told him to touch the sheriff even though I knew he'd see things that would probably give him nightmares for the rest of his life," Michael answered. "He thinks of the guy as his dad. Or at least he did."

One of the guards opened the door and Adam walked inside, his shoulders all hunched over like he was afraid someone was going to beat him up or something.

"I'm sorry," Michael said as soon as the door was locked behind Adam. "I'm sorry I had to make you play the game with Da—with Valenti. But you needed to know the truth about him. He's dangerous, Adam. This place is dangerous, for all of us."

Adam didn't answer for a moment. He didn't even blink. He just stared at Michael with his dead eyes. "Can we leave?" he finally asked.

"I think we might be able to," Michael answered. "But we'd need your help. Can you help us?"

Adam shuffled over and sat down in front of the cot. "I can help," he said.

"Okay, you remember how today we linked

with Bill and found out what his mother looked like?" Michael asked.

Adam nodded.

"We're going to do that with one of the guards. But instead of a mother, we're going to be looking for kids, okay? Go over and ask the guards if you can have something from your cell. When they go to get it, you and I will link. Then when the guard comes back and opens the door, you link with him and together we'll get a picture of his kids, okay?"

"Yeah," Adam answered softly. He got up and walked over to the door.

Cameron leaned close. "You think you can trust Pinky?" she asked.

"We'll see, won't we?" he answered, trying to ignore the smell of the beach coming off her. He couldn't get distracted.

Adam tapped on the glass, and a moment later the guard opened the door. "Could I have my cards?" Adam asked. "I forgot them."

"Why not?" The guard locked the door and headed off. Michael stood up and moved behind Adam. When the guard came back, Michael noticed that he moved one hand to his cattle prod before he opened the door again. Michael had been trying not to look suspicious, but obviously it didn't work. He moved back a step, careful to keep his fingers on Adam's arm.

Adam reached for the cards. The moment his

fingers touched the guard's, Michael was in. The two of them together really were powerful. Okay, kids, Michael thought. I need kids. The images blurred as they rushed past, then bam!—a little girl with dark braids and no front teeth appeared. Michael broke the connection and returned to the cot.

"Deal us a hand of crazy eights," Michael told Adam. He wanted everything to look nice and normal in the cell.

"Crazy eights?" Cameron repeated. But Michael spoke up before she could pursue.

"So, freaky girl, is there anything you can do to help us bust out of here?" Michael asked as he watched Adam lay out the cards.

"Sorry. I'm, uh, the experiments tapped me out. I did some other ones before they brought me into the lab with you guys," she answered.

"Okay, here's my plan, then," Michael began. "I can do this thing where I change people's appearances. Have you ever done that, Adam?" Adam shook his head. Cameron looked stunned. "I'm thinking that I'll make Cameron look like the guard's daughter. I'll threaten to kill you if they don't put down their weapons and let me lock them in here while we make a run for it."

"Maybe you're the one I should call Pinky," Cameron said. "The guard knows his daughter isn't in the compound."

"Yeah, his mind knows that. But what's his gut going to say when he sees his little girl in here? He's just going to want to save her, right?" Michael asked.

"I guess. Unless he's like my father," Cameron answered. "You know there will be other guards between here and the exit, don't you?"

"Yeah, but we'll still have our little girl hostage. And Adam and I have power." Michael shot a glance at Adam. It was very hard imagining him using his power to hurt anyone. It wasn't anything Michael would want him to have to do, either. The thought started the acid in his stomach churning.

"Maybe it would work better if I changed Adam's appearance," Michael said. As the hostage, Adam wouldn't have to hurt anyone. Michael would just have to hope he could handle any of the pain inflicting that came up. The way he was feeling right now, he might even enjoy it.

Michael moved down to the floor and sat across from Adam. "Move around so you can help me block the guards' view while I make the change," Michael told Cameron. She slid into place beside him.

"You ready?" Michael asked Adam. As soon as he nodded, Michael reached out and touched his face. "What I'm doing is moving the molecules around in your skin and bones to make you look like the little girl we saw. You can help me. Just focus on the molecules and squeeze them apart or push them together to make the changes."

The changes began happening so quickly that Michael could hardly register them all. Adam's hair darkened and grew longer. His cheekbones lowered. His front teeth disappeared.

Our power is more than doubled when we're linked, Michael realized as he and Adam completed the transformation in seconds, something that would have taken Michael fifteen or twenty minutes to do alone. He was definitely going to have to try some of this with Max and Isabel. If the three of them connected and used their powers . . . it was too mind-blowing to take in.

"You really are a freak," Cameron said, her voice shaky.

Michael shot her a look. "You're not going to faint on us or something, are you?"

"No way," she answered. "I don't want to spend the best years of my life singing that chain gang song. Let's blow this pop stand."

"Adam, when I grab you, all you have to do is scream your lungs out," Michael told him. He stood up and jerked Adam in front of him.

"Hey," Michael yelled. "If you want your daughter to live, drop the machine guns and the prods . . . now!"

Adam let out a shriek that Michael figured was only half faked.

"Stephanie," shouted the guard they had linked to.

"Yeah, we've got Stephanie," Cameron shouted. "Now put the weapons down and get in here, or get ready to say good-bye to your baby girl."

The guard they'd linked to dropped his machine gun. He threw down the cattle prod, unlocked the door, and rushed in.

"Your partner, too," Michael barked.

"Eaton, do it!" the guard in the cell cried.

Eaton hesitated. "I can kill with a touch," Michael yelled. "They told you that, right?"

"Eaton, they're going to kill my little girl!" the guard in the cell screeched.

Eaton threw down the machine gun and the prod and stepped into the cell.

"Get over to the cot, both of you," Michael ordered. When they obeyed, he backed out of the cell, still holding Adam in front of him. The second Cameron stepped through the doorway, he slammed the door shut and locked it.

"Which way out?" he cried.

"That's the way they brought me," Cameron answered, pointing. She scooped up one of the machine guns. "Come on!"

Michael didn't hesitate. He flew down the corridor after her, keeping his grip on Adam. She skidded to a stop in front of one of the huge metal doors. "We have to get through here!"

He didn't even bother with the molecules of the lock. He focused on the molecules of the door, *shoving* them together with his mind. The door screeched open with a hideous metallic crunching sound.

Cameron ducked through. Then Adam and Michael. And they were running again.

Earsplitting alarm bells started to ring. "I'll kill the little girl if I have to," Michael shouted, not even sure if anyone could hear him.

Cameron took a left, leading them into a long tunnel with a metal track down the center. "It's right down there," she yelled, her voice echoing.

This is actually going to work, Michael thought. The guards are holding back because they think we have the little girl. Although they'd probably figure it out in a few more seconds, as long as it took for Valenti to be informed.

"Okay, this is it," Cameron yelled. She slammed her fist against another metal door.

Michael concentrated and *shoved* it open. "Adam, you have to run. Run as hard as you can. If we get separated, go here." Michael made the connection, then sent Adam an image of the desert, then the town of Roswell and the Evanses' street, then Isabel and Max.

"Look out!" Cameron cried.

A metal grate slid back in the ceiling above them. A shot rang out. Cameron yelled in pain, and the machine gun fell from her hands. A fraction of a second later a guard swung down and grabbed her.

"Adam, go!" Michael cried. Then he lunged for the guard.

"Move, and I kill her," the guard yelled.

Michael froze. Out of the corner of his eye he caught sight of Adam just outside the doorway. What was he doing? Why wasn't he moving?

"Adam, run!" Cameron screamed.

"You have to leave us. Go, go, go!" Michael shouted.

Adam hesitated, staring out into the night. It was too big, too empty. He couldn't go out there and live. It would swallow him up. He'd disappear.

"Now!" Michael yelled.

And Adam's feet were moving, flying across the desert floor. He stared down at them, only at them. It's as if they were moving without his control. Following Michael's order whether he wanted them to or not.

Left, right. Left, right. Taking him away. Away from Michael. Away from home. Away from everything he knew.

His body changed as he ran, his little bird legs lengthening, his feet spreading out, allowing him to run faster. Left, right. Left, right. Something coming up in front of him. Cactus. He'd seen it in a book that Dad had given him.

Not Dad anymore. Swerve. Run. And don't look up. Don't ever look up.

His heart pounded in his chest, in his ears, the beat picking up speed. He pushed himself to run faster, matching his stride to the thuds of his heart.

Adam kept his eyes locked on his feet, allowing his mind to go blank, his world narrowed down to the patch of desert directly in front of him. Rock. Jump. Left, right. Left, right. Don't look up.

Mesquite bush. Swerve. Too late. Adam's left foot tangled in it and he went down hard, sand scratching his cheek and getting in his mouth.

Adam lay there for a moment until he felt his heart slow down a little. Then he sat up. And the sky filled his vision, stretching outward to the horizon and beyond. Endless in every direction. The stars so far away. Farther than his mind could comprehend.

He shivered. He realized the air around him was cold. He'd never experienced cold before. Not like this. He'd washed his face and hands with cold water, yes. But the air at the compound was perfectly controlled. Always the same.

Adam curled his knees up to his chest, hugging himself. He felt a little warmer, a tiny bit better.

But it was still too big, too empty. He squeezed his eyes shut to block out the sky. And he tried to stay very, very still.

Maria snapped open the plastic box of the *Treachery and Greed on the Planet of the Apes* video, then snapped it shut again and tossed it onto her night table. When she'd seen the movie on the shelf at the video store, she'd thought it was the perfect choice. But now she realized she only wanted to watch it if Michael was there to watch it with her.

Except even if Michael was back home, it's not like he'd necessarily come crawling through her window for a movie marathon. That kind of thing was probably reserved for the buddy Maria, not the Maria who exposed her guts and actually told Michael she loved him.

You don't know that, she told herself.

Do too.

Do not.

Do too. Do not. Do too.

The conflicting thoughts ricocheted through her brain until she wanted to scream. Then she heard something that instantly stopped her debate with herself—the sound of her window sliding up. Michael!

Maria sprang up from her bed and yanked her curtains back. Alex gave her a sheepish grin. "I broke that troll thing next to the back gate," he admitted. He peered up at her, his eyebrows drawing together. "I'm sorry. You really liked it, huh?" he added.

"That thing! No. Ick. It's hideous," she said quickly, trying to get the oh-God-I-really-wanted-you-to-be-someone-else expression off her face so as not to make Alex think she'd been struck by troll grief. She grabbed his hand and helped him through the window. "A guy my mom was going out with gave it to her, but she's about three guys past him now. Maybe you should do one of your lists on how not to impress a woman. Giving her a ceramic troll is up there."

"So, presents, they're pretty important, huh?" Alex asked. He shoved off his sneakers and flopped down on Maria's bed. "Oh, it's okay that I came over, isn't it?"

Maria sat down next to him. "Definitely," she answered.

"So if I didn't give the right present or, actually, any present, that would be—," Alex began.

"No. No, I meant it's definitely okay that you came over," she interrupted. "Not definitely that presents are important. Although they're nice, I guess."

"Isabel gave me a present once," Alex said. "Want to see?"

"Sure." Maria wriggled closer, finding the fact that Isabel had given Alex a present very cool. Maybe she was totally wrong about Isabel getting a thing for Michael.

Alex pulled out his wallet and slid out a strip of pictures from one of those little photo booths. He handed it to Maria. "When she gave that to me, she said she was thinking about me in every picture," he explained.

Who would have guessed Isabel had a squishy, lovey-dovey marshmallow heart? Maria thought, smiling. Apparently she was wrong about Isabel losing interest in Alex because of that dream of Michael's. Maria had been so sure that dream had started Isabel thinking of Michael in a different way. But maybe not.

Except wait. Alex said Isabel gave him a present *once*.

"Um, when did Isabel give you this?" Maria asked.

Please let it be postdream, she thought. Please, please, please.

"Not that long after Nikolas died," Alex answered.

Predream. Great.

"And today she dumped me. I just don't get it," Alex continued.

"Wait. She dumped you? Why didn't you tell me?" Maria demanded.

"I just did," Alex said.

Guys. They just don't get it, she thought. He'd been in her room for at least three full minutes, and he was just telling her this now?

Maybe she should just be thankful for the scoop. Now she knew for sure that Isabel had dumped Alex because of her feelings for Michael.

Maria studied the little strip of photos. God, Isabel was beautiful. Yeah, they both had blond hair and blue eyes, plus arms and legs and stuff. But on Isabel everything just worked together perfectly. There was no way Maria could compete.

Alex reached over and pulled the photos out of her fingers.

"Talk to me. What happened?" Maria asked.

"You saw how she was at our meeting, right?" Alex scrubbed his face with his fingers. "She was kind of jumping down my throat whenever I said anything. Then afterward I said something like how I knew she was feeling upset about Michael. I mean, girls are supposed to like it when you try and figure out how they're feeling, right?" He glanced at Maria for confirmation.

"Yeah. Of course," she answered.

"Well, not Isabel. She just exploded. She was all, like, 'You don't have any right to know what I think.'"

Poor Alex. He sounded kind of dazed, like a guy who'd been in a car crash and was wandering around the highway, talking about the milk he was supposed to pick up on his way home. No clue where he was or even what had really happened.

"Hey, you want some cedar?" she asked, reaching for her collection of aromatherapy vials. It was the only comforting thing she could think of to say. "It will make you feel better."

"The only way it would make me feel better is if you gave me a big vat of it so I could stick my head in and drown myself," Alex answered.

I know the feeling, Maria thought.

"I was going to nuke some popcorn, but, uh, I can't remember how long I have to leave it in, or, um, if it's supposed to be on high or what," Max said.

Isabel shook her head at him. "Just push that little button that says popcorn," she answered. "Now, I have a question for you."

Max leaned against the door frame, half in and half out of her room. "Okay, so ask."

"What do you really want?" Isabel said.

A faint blush colored Max's cheeks. You are just too nice, my brother, Isabel thought. She didn't know how Max was going to make it in the big, bad world when he couldn't even pull off a little lie, like pretending he couldn't make popcorn.

"I just heard some yelling before, uh, around when Alex was leaving," he said.

Oooh, very subtle.

"Come on. Let's go get popcorn." Isabel stood up and pushed her way past him. "I was a total jerk," she blurted out as they started down the stairs.

Max didn't answer. "This is the part where you're supposed to say that there's no way I could ever be a jerk of any kind," she told him, shooting a glance over her shoulder.

"But Isabel, there's no way you could ever—," he obediently began.

"Oh, forget it," she said as she led the way into the kitchen. "We both know that's not true. If you asked everyone at school to come up with one word that would describe me, you know what it would be."

"Now, that's definitely not true," Max answered. "It might make the top ten, but there's no way it would be number one."

Isabel grabbed a bag of popcorn out of the kitchen cabinet, stuck it in the microwave, and hit the button. She stared through the little window. Not that watching the bag expand was all that fascinating. It's just that it was hard to have this conversation and actually look at Max at the same time. Admitting that she'd done anything wrong wasn't Isabel's style. Confessing that she'd treated Alex, a guy she actually cared about, like dog poop was almost impossible.

"Okay, maybe it wouldn't be number one on everyone's list. But on Alex's, definitely." Isabel leaned closer to the little window. She thought maybe the microwave light was too bright because her eyes were starting to sting.

Yeah, you keep telling yourself that, baby, she thought. It's the light. Because there's no way you would cry over Alex, the guy *you* gave the boot.

"Alex knows you're really stressed about Michael," Max told her. She heard him pull out one of the kitchen chairs and sit down. "I'm sure if you called him up and said you were sorry about whatever went down, he'd be fine with it."

"Even if I broke up with him?" Isabel asked.

"You broke up with Alex?" Max yelped. The kernels of popcorn started to explode.

"Yeah, and I wasn't exactly *sensitive* about it, either," Isabel said, still talking to the microwave.

"Why?" Max asked. "You know what," he said before she could answer, "it doesn't really matter. You want him back, right? Just call and say that."

Isabel waited until the popping died down, then she pulled out the bag and ripped it open. The hot steam burned her fingers as she grabbed a basket off the top of the fridge and dumped the popcorn in. "The thing is, I don't think I do. Want him back, I mean," Isabel admitted.

She turned around and shoved the basket of popcorn down in front of Max. She grabbed a handful and stuffed it into her mouth, an un-popped kernel singeing her tongue, making her eyes water again.

"Oh." Max crammed a huge wad of popcorn into his mouth, and they both just crunched for a minute.

Isabel knew what Max's next question would be—why didn't she want him back? Good question. Alex was smart, funny, cute. Not exactly the crème de la crème of high school high society. But still. He'd gotten her through some bad times, really bad times.

But now whenever she was with him, she was thinking about someone else.

How could she tell her brother that she'd gone into Michael's dream and seen him with his arms around her? How could she explain that had changed everything?

She couldn't tell Max the raw truth—that recently, every time Alex kissed her, Isabel wondered what it would have felt like if Michael had done the kissing. Yeah, she and Max were pretty close. But he was still her brother. And this wasn't really something she could talk about to a brother, especially because Michael was Max's best friend, practically a part of the family. She thought it might give Max the wiggins to think of Michael and his sister like that.

"Did you hear something?" Max asked. He

jumped up and peered out the kitchen window. "I think somebody's out there."

"I didn't hear a car, so it can't be Mom and Dad," Isabel answered. A bolt of pure hope sizzled through her. Michael? She raced to the front door and dashed outside, Max right behind her.

She saw a figure lying on the front lawn, looking half dead. "Michael!" she screamed. She flew over and dropped to her knees next to him.

But it wasn't Michael. It was some guy she'd never seen before. About her age. Green, sad eyes. His harsh, ragged breathing. He was really pale.

Max crouched down next to her. He reached out and gently shook the guy's shoulder. "Are you okay?" he asked. "What in the . . ."

Isabel jerked up her head as Max's voice trailed away. She saw his eyes widen, then a horrified expression spread across his face.

"Max, what?" she demanded.

He didn't answer.

"What?" she yelled, jerking his hand away from the guy.

"You're not going to believe this. I think he's one of us," Max told her. "I connected the second I touched him. I saw a pod like ours." He swallowed hard. "I saw Valenti. A glass cell. I think . . . I think he's from the compound."

Isabel felt all the little hairs on the back of her neck stand on end. "How did he survive it?" she

79

whispered. He had lived her worst fear—being held prisoner at Sheriff Valenti's mercy.

The guy's eyes flickered open, but an instant later he squeezed them shut again. "Too big," he whimpered. "Too big."

"Let's get him inside," Max said. He slid his arm under the guy and helped him to his feet. Isabel took the other side, wrapping her arm around his waist. She could feel the guy's tremors as she and Max walked him toward the house.

"You're with us now," Isabel said fiercely. "We're not going to let anything hurt you again."

Max led the way to the booth in the back corner of Flying Pepperoni, where he had told Liz and Isabel to meet him. It was less crowded back there, but Max was still worried about Adam. He was getting his I'm-about-to-freak expression again.

And Max didn't blame him. It hadn't even been twenty-four hours since Adam had escaped, and he'd already done more new things than most people did in a year. Even stuff as basic as a toaster was strange and amazing to Adam. Yeah, he'd seen pictures of toasters in a book, but he'd never actually used one. He'd loved the popping sound. Max bet between the two of them they'd eaten a loaf of toast that day. Max would have eaten even more, just to witness Adam's pure joy.

"We'll sit here and wait for everyone else to show up," Max told Adam as he slid into the booth. Adam slid in across from him. "So, how are you doing? Do you, uh, have any questions or anything?"

"Not really," Adam answered. He closed his eyes and slid closer to the wall of the booth.

Yeah, he was getting very close to the freak-out

zone. Max did a visual sweep of the restaurant. I could use a little help here, guys, he thought. As if in reply to this thought, he saw Liz's grinning face walk through the restaurant.

"Uh, Adam." Max waited for Adam to open his eyes, then continued. "This is Liz. I told you about her, remember?"

"Hi," Adam said nervously. Liz sat next to Max. Adam looked at her and squeezed his eyes shut again.

Liz shot Max a worried look, then she pulled open her bag, rooted around, and pulled out the sunglasses she wore with her *Men in Black*–style uniform when she was waitressing. She reached across the table and gently slid the glasses on him. He jerked back, startled. "Try opening your eyes now. Everything will look a little less . . . intense."

Adam glanced around. Max felt himself relax a bit. Maybe Liz had found a way for Adam to be out in public without risking a meltdown.

"Hey, Adam. I've been thinking about you all day," Isabel said as she hurried up to the booth. She slid in next to him. "How did it go? What did you and Max do?"

Max noticed that with Adam, his sister dropped all her I-am-Princess-Isabel-and-all-must-worship-me garbage. She treated him so tenderly, it was almost bizarre to watch.

"We made toast," Adam answered. "And Max taught me how to play poker."

"Great, Max. Toast and poker. I'm glad you covered the essentials. I knew I should have been the one to stay home with him," Isabel said. "You talked to Adam about not using power, right?"

"Yeah." Max's stomach tightened as he remembered that little conversation. "Adam, um, Adam didn't realize that he comes from another place. He didn't realize that most people here can't do the things he can do."

"What *does* he know?" Isabel asked.

Max explained what he'd covered with Adam—that he and Isabel and Michael and Adam all came from the same planet and that they were probably the only people on earth who did come from there. And he'd told Adam that he shouldn't tell anyone this or use his powers. And then there were all the little things—like toast and poker—that Adam had never seen.

But Max hadn't told Adam what would happen if he did tell people the truth. He didn't tell him that most people would be afraid of him. Or that some would hate him. Or that some would want to kill him. Max knew he'd have to explain this to Adam sometime soon. But not now. He had enough to deal with.

"Here come Maria and Alex," Liz said. She scooted closer to Max to make room, and he looped his arm around her shoulders, just like a normal guy. Max never thought he'd be able to have this, to have a girl—a human girl—know the truth about him and still love him.

I should tell Adam about me and Liz, he thought. He should know that just because he's *different* doesn't mean he doesn't get any of the good stuff.

Maria went to sit by Liz, but Alex hooked her by the arm. "Sit here," he said, nodding toward the spot next to Isabel. An awkward silence lingered as Maria looked at Alex, confused. Postbreakup weirdness, Max thought. They sat down.

"Adam, this is Alex. And that's Maria," Max told him. "If you need anything, you can come to any of us. You can talk to any of us about anything. You can ask us any questions. You can—"

"You can trust us," Alex interrupted.

"Yeah, that basically covers it. You can trust us," Max agreed.

Adam didn't say anything. He had to be on complete overload. "We need to decide what to do with Adam," Max went on. "Who we're going to say he is, where he's going to live, what he's going to do for—"

Max stopped himself. He was talking like Adam wasn't even there. He had to keep reminding himself that even though Adam acted sort of like a little kid, he wasn't. "Sorry, Adam," he said. "I didn't mean to make it sound like we were just going to decide everything for you. It's just that you're pretty much walking into a whole new world."

"Yeah. It's a place we've lived in all our lives. So we know the basic stuff that you need to get by," Maria added. "Do you think we could say he was an exchange student? If we did, maybe he could just live with us." She turned toward Adam. "An exchange student is someone from another country who comes to live and go to school in a different place for a while."

"Like on TV," Adam said.

"They didn't have TV in the compound, so I was teaching him how to channel surf," Max explained.

"What a mentor," Isabel said, smiling.

"I don't know if the exchange student thing would really work. I mean, where would we say he was from?" Max said.

"Delaware?" Alex joked. Isabel flashed him an annoyed look. "Just kidding. You know, *kidding*," Alex said.

"We could always take him to the cave," Max offered.

"I don't want him so far away. Not all alone," Isabel answered, her voice rough with emotion.

"We have this little shed out in the backyard that he could stay in until we figure out something better," Liz told them. "It has electricity and everything because once for two seconds my dad thought he wanted to do carpentry and he bought all these electric tools."

"What do you think, Adam? Would you mind living there?" Max asked. "You'd have to stay out of sight when Liz's parents are around."

Adam looked over at Liz. "I would be close to you?"

"Totally close. I could be out to the shed in three seconds if you needed me," she promised him.

"That sounds good," he answered, a slow smile spreading across his face.

Max had felt that same kind of goofy smile on his own face when he looked at Liz. He tried to imagine what it would be like to go sixteen years without ever seeing a girl your own age and then to suddenly be surrounded by them. It might be kind of scary, but fun scary. At least Adam had Liz, Maria, and Izzy to be his training-wheel girls.

"I'm starving. Does anyone actually work here, or are we supposed to take our own order and then make ourselves a pizza?" Alex asked.

"Lucinda Baker is working today. One of you guys take off your shirt. That will get her back here fast enough," Isabel said.

Adam started to tug off his sweatshirt. "No, no. I was just kidding, Adam," Isabel said, stopping him midstrip. The entire table broke into laughter.

"Lucinda! If you want anything approaching a tip, get back here," she yelled. Lucinda appeared almost immediately.

"So what do we want?" Alex asked. "Adam, what's your favorite?"

"I don't know," Adam answered, tensing up a little.

"They never let him choose his food," Max told Alex. The second the words were out of his mouth, he realized it was a stupid thing to say.

"He just got out of one of those really strict boarding schools," Liz jumped in.

"Oooh, you must have been a bad boy," Lucinda teased. "I like bad boys."

Uh-oh. Now, Lucinda, she definitely wasn't a training-wheels girl. She had a whole home page on the web describing the kissing technique of the guys at school that made it very clear she had some pretty high standards. She'd eat little Adam alive.

Before Max had a chance to decide what he should be doing about this Lucinda-Adam situation, Lucinda reached out and ran her fingers down Adam's cheek, her screaming red nails looking even brighter against his pale skin. By the enthralled look on Adam's face, Max knew he had connected with her. He's got to get out of that habit, Max thought.

Adam gave a little jerk. "I like that underwear you have," he told Lucinda. "The brown ones with the white squiggly lines. It reminds me of a cupcake."

Max covered his face with his hands. Isabel laughed out loud.

"Hey, how did you know about my underwear?" Lucinda demanded.

Okay, think fast, Max ordered himself. You don't want Adam ending up in the circus. Or with his own nine hundred number.

"Oh, Lucinda, come on," Isabel answered, before Max could formulate some kind of excuse. "You have shown way too many guys your underwear to ask that question. You know how guys like to brag."

"You know what? Could we get that pizza to go?" Max asked.

9

"So, do you want to play truth or dare?" Cameron asked. She leaned back against the glass wall of his cell.

"Do I look like a junior high school girl to you?" Michael answered, although he was already thinking of some pretty interesting ways the game could go.

"Oh, come on," Cameron begged, bouncing her head against the glass. "I'm so bored."

"If you keep doing that, you'll give yourself enough brain damage that you'll never be bored again," he answered. She shot him an annoyed look. "Okay, okay," he relented. "What's the most embarrassing thing that you've ever done? Truth or dare."

"You're supposed to ask if I'm a virgin. That's always the first question," Cameron teased.

"So are you?" Michael asked. Yeah, it was definitely going to be an interesting game.

"Too late," she said. "You already asked something. Most embarrassing, most embarrassing. Let's see . . ."

"Too many to pick from, huh?" Michael asked. He stretched out on the floor, propping himself up with his elbow.

"Okay, I got it. I was at this party. I was about twelve, I think. And I don't know why, but we ended up doing this thing where we got in pairs and had to look into the other person's eyes for a full minute without talking." Cameron took a deep breath and rushed on. "So anyway, my partner was Sean Wentworth, this guy I had a total crush on. We started looking at each other, and I don't know exactly what happened, I guess I just got nervous, because I barfed and some of it splattered on him."

Michael cracked up. He could totally picture it.

"It wasn't funny," Cameron said. "I'd been pigging out at the party, and there were these lumps of half-digested pizza and chicken wings and stuff in there. It wasn't one of those nice, all-liquid deals."

Michael laughed harder. The story seemed like something Maria might tell him. Not Isabel, though. No way. If Isabel ever had a most embarrassing moment, she definitely wouldn't describe it down to the lumps of half-digested pizza.

"If you could manage to stop laughing at me, it's my turn," Cameron told him.

"Go ahead," he said, struggling to control himself.

"So are you a virgin? Truth or dare," Cameron asked.

"Dare," Michael answered without hesitation.

"You realize you answered the question, whether you think you did or not?" Cameron informed him. "Any guy who wasn't a virgin would be totally bragging about it."

He felt his face getting warm. If I'm blushing, then I know for sure what my most embarrassing moment is, he thought.

"I'm one of those sensitive kind of guys who respects women way too much to ever do anything as crude as bragging," Michael said quickly. "Not that I don't have things I *could* brag about."

"Ooohh. I'll bet you have all kinds of stories about lusty hookups, adoring female fans, and championship football games," Cameron snapped. "Am I right there, cowboy?"

"My turn. What's the worst thing you've ever done? Truth or dare," Michael asked.

Cameron pulled in a sharp breath, and her entire body tensed up.

Way to break the mood, Guerin. Michael shoved his hands through his spiky black hair.

"I'll take a dare," Cameron said.

This didn't seem like the moment to ask to see her tattoos. "Uh, all right, you have to look into my eyes for one minute without puking," Michael told her.

"You like to live dangerously, don't you?"

Michael was happy to see that the tightness in

Cameron's body was already starting to go away. He sat up and moved closer until his knees were almost touching hers, then they locked eyes.

He'd always thought he went for blue eyes, like Maria's and Isabel's. But Cameron's brown eyes were pretty amazing. For one thing, they weren't just brown. Or at least not all the same shade of brown.

Michael leaned closer, so close, he could feel Cameron's breath against his face. Her eyes weren't plain brown at all. Right around the pupil there was a little ring of dark chocolatey brown, with sort of an uneven edge. Then most of her eye was a lighter sort of caramel brown, with a really, really thin ring of the dark brown around it.

"Has it been a minute yet?" Cameron asked.

Michael wasn't sure. All he knew was that even if it had been twice that long, he wasn't ready to move away. He moved a fraction nearer, the distance between them practically nonexistent now.

And she pulled away. Jerked away was more like it.

"That was definitely a minute," Cameron said, her voice all shaky. "My turn. Do you ever wish you weren't an alien? Truth or dare."

Michael stared at her. He couldn't believe she was tackling this "forbidden" topic.

"It seemed like we'd decided not to talk about our assorted freakishness," Cameron hurried to say.

"I don't even know why I asked that question. I'll give you a different one."

"No, it's too late. You already asked it." Michael had never talked much to humans about that part of himself. It's not like he thought Maria, or Liz, or Alex would get all weird about it. He just never felt like it, that's all.

But why shouldn't he answer Cameron's questions? As she said, they were both freaks. So he should be able to tell her anything, right?

Adam clicked off the TV. It was fake, and he hated fake. His whole pathetic life had been fake—from believing that the sun was only something in storybooks to believing Valenti was his father.

He checked the watch that Alex had given him. Almost an hour before school got out. Almost an hour until he would be allowed to go out into the real world. *Allowed.* Max, Isabel, and the others didn't carry machine guns, but they still wanted to be his guards. Don't go outside unless one of us is with you, Adam. Don't talk to anyone but us, Adam.

They gave him a TV, a CD player, and real books instead of those picture books Valenti had made him read. But was he supposed to get all excited over a bunch of fake stuff? Should he be happy in his little shed world, kept away from everything real?

He wanted real. He wanted a girl—a girl as pretty as Liz—spinning around on the grass, her head flung back, her arms open wide, her long hair swirling around her. He wanted his own toes in that same grass. He wanted his fingers touching her face.

The more he thought, the antsier he became. Why wait any longer for the real world when he could get a taste of it—right now? He stood up and rushed over to the shed door. He grabbed the handle and froze. Could he really just walk out?

The thought felt shocking. Revolutionary. Miraculous.

Adam flung open the door. Sunny blue sky filled with heaps of fluffy clouds exploded above him. He started to feel a little dizzy, and he wobbled on his feet. He thought about putting on his sunglasses to take the edge off. But no. This was real. This was what he wanted. Straight-up reality.

He crossed the lawn to the back gate, hurried through and slammed it behind him, then headed to the sidewalk and made a left. He had no real plan, but he vaguely remembered that left would take him to the center of town.

As he walked, he was bombarded with new sensations, his knowledge of the real world expanding with every step. He'd seen pictures of ginkgo trees, but now he discovered the sharp, sour smell of the fleshy yellow seeds and the feel of veins in the scalloped leaves. He'd seen cars on TV, but for the first time he smelled the exhaust and felt the little whoosh of air when one passed close by.

He could practically feel his brain growing. He had the feeling that he was becoming more real as his experience of the real world increased.

Turning onto North Main Street, Adam saw a whole row of the fast-food places he'd seen advertised on TV. He could eat anything he wanted, anytime he wanted. That was, if he had any money.

He stopped at the corner, listening to the clicking sound as the streetlight changed. Another new thing. When the little walking pedestrian lit up, he crossed the street. He felt like giggling. It was so hard to believe he was really up here. He couldn't decide whether to look in the store windows, at the other people on the street, or at some more cars, so he kept turning his head back and forth, trying to watch everything at once.

Then he spotted a sign in the pawn shop window that said Live Alien Inside, and that captured his attention. What was this? Max had made it very clear that Adam could never tell anyone that he was from another planet. He'd said that's the reason Valenti had kept Adam in the compound.

Adam cautiously stepped into the store, scanning the narrow aisles. He saw a woman behind the counter. Was she the alien? Was he even allowed to ask that?

"Can I help you with something?" she called.

Adam slowly approached her. "Uh, I saw that sign in the window."

She grinned. "And you wanted to see the alien. Be right back." She turned around and ducked through the curtain behind her. A moment later she reappeared, carrying a spider monkey. At least it looked exactly like the spider monkeys he'd seen in the big book of animals he'd had in the compound. "His name is Scooter," she said.

"That's an alien?" Adam asked.

"No, it's just a joke. You know, to get people into the place. Everyone knows aliens look like this." She patted a green plastic head next to the cash register.

The thing looked evil, skeletal with huge almond-shaped eyes. "I have a friend who was abducted," the woman continued, "and I have to put this thing away every time she comes in. She says the guys who took her looked exactly like this." She reached below the counter and pulled out a rifle. "All I have to say is, if they try to come after me, they're going to get quite a welcome."

Adam backed up a few steps, then he turned around and made for the door. He took huge gulps of the fresh air as he hurried down the street. Reality had just taken a very strange turn.

Was that how most humans saw aliens? As horrible things that were going to come and get them? Things they had to shoot on sight? Was it true? Were there aliens like that?

The questions bubbled in his brain. He checked his watch. He looked up and noticed that place, that eating place where Liz worked. Liz should be at work.

He picked up his pace as he continued down the street, going faster and faster until he was running. He'd feel better when he saw Liz. She could explain how humans really felt about aliens.

But that wasn't the only reason he wanted to see her. There was something about Liz. He wasn't sure what to call it. When he was around her, he felt one hundred percent real.

"Have you seen Adam?" Max demanded.

"He wasn't in the shed?" Liz cried. She dropped the sponge she'd been using to wipe down the café's counter.

"Would I be asking if you'd—" Max stopped himself. "No, I just came from there. Was he in the shed before school? When's the last time you saw him?"

"I brought some breakfast to him this morning.

97

And I told him you would be there as soon as you could," Liz answered.

What was he thinking, leaving Adam alone? It was only his second day out of the compound. Third, if you counted the first night. Two, three, it didn't matter. Adam was like a little kid. Max wouldn't have left a little kid by himself.

"Max, whatever you're thinking, stop it," Liz demanded, her voice harsh. "You can't take responsibility for everything. It's insane."

Sometimes he hated the way she always seemed to know what he was thinking.

Maria rushed up. "What's wrong? I could tell there was something wrong all the way across the room. One of you start talking."

"Adam wasn't in the shed," Liz said. "Maria, a guy at table four is waving his coffee cup."

"Pretend you don't see him," Maria answered. "He's had way too much caffeine already. So what are we going to do about Adam?"

"How has he been acting?" Max asked Liz. "Do you think he could have decided to take off?"

"No, I don't think so. He's been excited and curious—like a little kid. Yesterday morning, he picked some gardenias and asked me what they were. I explained that they were flowers—living things—and that we would have to put them in water before they died. He felt terrible. It was so cute." Liz said, smiling.

"So, do you think he left the shed to go out and explore?" Maria asked.

"Yeah, maybe. There was one weird thing that happened. He asked if he could touch my face, because he had never touched a girl—"

"So you let him?" Max asked impatiently.

"Yeah, I let him. It didn't seem creepy, just innocent," Liz said. "Afterward I told him—firmly—that he couldn't just go around touching people. And he reacted kind of strangely, like I had scolded him. Do you think maybe it hurt his feelings or something?"

"I don't think so," Maria said.

"I don't know," Liz said. "He's not really used to—"

"Well, you can ask him yourself because he just walked in," Maria interrupted. "The bad news is that he's with Elsevan DuPris."

"Oh, great. Just perfect," Max muttered. "Now DuPris will have a great story for his ridiculous alien paper. 'I Had Dinner with an Alien.'"

"That's actually kind of tame. The *Astral Projector* would probably give it a title like, 'An Alien Ate My Brains for Dinner,'" Maria said. Then she winced. "Sorry. Just nervous."

"I'm going to go over there and see if I can tell if Adam has said anything we need to worry about," Liz told them.

"What excuse are you going to use? For going up to them, I mean?" Maria asked.

"Uh, I thought I'd disguise myself as a waitress," Liz answered.

"Sorry. Just really nervous," Maria said.

Max watched Liz cross the restaurant. He couldn't help noticing that Adam's eyes were locked on her. He wasn't even blinking.

"It's a crush," Maria told him. "You know, like the one you had on that girl Raina freshman year."

Max watched Liz turn the charm on DuPris, getting him to talk. And he watched Adam watching Liz. That is so not important right now, he told himself. You can talk to Adam about Liz later. But his eyes kept going to Adam, and he felt relieved when Liz headed back toward him.

"We have nothing to worry about," Liz reported when she got back to Max and Maria. "DuPris is off on one of his southern-fried tangents. Telling one of his amusing stories about drinking mint julep with grandpap. No alien talk at all."

"We still have to get Adam out of here," Max said. "What if Valenti happens to drive by or something?"

Liz pulled her order pad out of her pocket. "All I need is an order of spaghetti with extra sauce."

"Okay, I know I'm the queen of the dim today, but why?" Maria asked.

"Oh, come on. You know how clumsy I am," Liz answered.

Maria smiled. "Ah, the old spaghetti-in-the-lap

trick. An extreme but effective tactic. You haven't used it in a while."

"You've done this before?" Max asked.

"Only when some way too friendly guy tries to slip a tip in my pocket—from the inside," Liz told him. She grabbed a water pitcher and started back toward Adam and DuPris.

From the inside. That meant—

"Here, smell this." Maria thrust one of her aromatherapy vials into his hand. "It's great for getting rid of feelings of jealousy."

Max rolled the vial between his fingers as he watched Adam watching Liz. "I'm not sure it's going to be enough."

"Maybe we should use the rest of the drive time to go over some basic, not rules, but, you know, normal behavior stuff," Liz suggested.

Isabel shot another look at Adam. He didn't seem to be offended. She wondered if he even got what Liz meant. He wasn't stupid or anything, but he'd just had so little experience.

"Yeah, Adam," Max said. "Remember what I told you about using your powers? You can't connect to people except us, okay? People don't like it if you know things about them they haven't actually told you."

"I have one," Maria jumped in. "No matter what, you must always leave the toilet seat up after you pee. If you don't, people will get suspicious."

"Don't mess with his head like that," Isabel told her.

"I'm not. I'm trying to help him figure out what typical guy behavior is," Maria protested.

"What else?" Adam asked. "I need to know this stuff."

Isabel smiled. Adam was starting to talk a little more. He must be starting to feel more secure around them.

"Okay, Maria's right," Isabel said. "Most guys leave the seat up. *But* if you want to be the kind of guy who is able to, say, attract a girl, then you should resist your natural guy instincts and put the seat down."

"What else?" Alex asked, without looking at her. "I'm curious to know what else a guy needs to do to attract a girl."

Aw, someone needs a Band-Aid for his poor trampled feelings, Isabel thought. Then she immediately felt bad. She'd been kind of relieved that yesterday's fight had exploded into a breakup, but it's not like she was happy that she'd hurt him.

"Come on, Isabel. I really want to know," Alex said.

Isabel promised herself she'd say *something* to Alex later, some kind of it's-not-you-it's-me thing to try and take away some of the bad feeling between them. But she wasn't going to do it in front of everyone.

"All right," she answered. "If you want to be a typical guy, fart whenever you want and then make some stupid joke about it, like, 'I'll have to stop feeding the dog so much cheese.' But if you want to be the other kind of guy, one who actually can get a girl, leave the room when you have to do that kind of thing."

Was that a satisfying answer? Isabel wondered.

"We're here," Max said. He pulled the Jeep to a stop. "Adam, Alex and I will tell you all the guy behavior stuff later, when there are no girls around."

Isabel climbed out and grabbed the tan tarp from under the backseat. She helped Max cover the Jeep so that it wouldn't attract any attention.

"There's something I want to ask," Adam said as they all started hiking over to the cave entrance.

"Yeah, anything," Max said.

"What's going to happen to Michael?"

"We're going to get him out," Isabel promised. "We've just been waiting for the right time."

"I want to help," Adam said.

"We need you to," Alex answered. "The thing that would help the most right now is for you to tell us everything you can about the compound. The more we know about the layout, the better plan we'll be able to come up with."

"Will it make you feel bad to talk about it?" Maria asked, before Isabel could ask the same question.

"No, it's okay." Adam adjusted his sunglasses. "Michael's cell is in one big room that has a bunch of other cells, too."

Isabel assumed that Michael had been kept in a cell or a cage or something. But hearing Adam say it sucked all the air out of her lungs.

"Are any of the other cells occupied?" Alex asked.

"Only one. There's this girl, Cameron," Adam answered.

"A girl?" Maria asked. "Who is she? Why is she there?"

"I don't know. She got there right after Michael. Da—Sheriff Valenti brought her in. The doctor made her do stuff with us."

"What kind of stuff?" Isabel demanded.

"Like breaking things without touching them," Adam answered. "Or saying what number card the doctor was holding."

"Do you think she could have been one of us? From a different planet, I mean?" Max asked.

"I don't know," Adam answered, his voice strained. "I don't know anything."

"That's not your fault," Alex said.

"This crack in the ground leads to the cave," Max explained to Adam. "You can just swing yourself down. There's a big rock pretty much right below the opening that you can feel with your toes."

Adam scrambled down with ease. Isabel followed him. It felt so strange to be in the cave without Michael. It had always been more his place than anyone's. He'd spent a lot of nights out here when he couldn't deal with one of his assorted foster homes.

"What else can you tell us about the compound?" Max asked Adam after they were all settled. "How many guards are there?"

"There are always two guards outside the cells. There are always guards in the lab, too. And guards escorted me, and Michael, and Cameron everywhere. We were never alone."

"Do you know how many exits there are?" Alex asked.

"I think maybe I could find the one I came out of, but that's all I know," Adam answered, starting to sound angry at himself again.

"We can stake out the area around the compound and see if we can find any other entrances," Isabel said.

"Maybe we should check out Valenti's house," Alex said. "Maybe he has something on his computer or some paperwork that would give us info about the guards' schedules and maybe even some more details about the architecture of the compound."

"Before we launch into a major planning session, I have to go outside for a minute," Max said.

"We just got here," Isabel protested.

"I bet he has to feed the dog some cheese," Alex joked. He stood up. "I'm going, too. I have to take advantage of the lack of toilet seats."

Maria rolled her eyes. "Guys," she muttered.

Talking about the compound was making Isabel tense. She stood up and wandered around the cave, trying to work out a little nervous energy. She stopped dead when she spotted Michael's jacket lying on top of his sleeping bag.

She knelt down and lifted the jacket up to her face, pulling in a deep breath. It still smelled like him. She slid the jacket on and wrapped her arms around herself. For just one moment she wanted to pretend that they were Michael's arms around her, making her feel safe the way nothing else could.

Isabel heard a scuffling sound behind her. She turned around and saw Maria.

"I—" Maria shifted her weight from foot to foot. "I heard about you and Alex, and I just wanted to say I'm sorry. You guys seemed like a good couple."

"Thanks," Isabel murmured. She didn't want to talk right now. She wanted to hold on to the fantasy that Michael was really there with her.

"Was it . . ." Maria hesitated. "Is it something you think you'll be able to fix?"

Isabel shook her head. She shoved her hands in the pockets of the jacket. Maria just kept standing there.

She's thinking about that dream of Michael's we

both saw, Isabel finally realized. *She's wondering if I broke up with Alex because I want to be with Michael.*

Isabel wasn't really used to having girlfriends yet. But she was pretty sure that when you knew one of your girlfriends had a crush—a life-threatening crush like the one Maria had on Michael—you weren't supposed to go after the guy yourself.

Maria's friendship was important to her. More important than she could have imagined a few months ago. But Michael. Isabel had to at least find out what would happen if they kissed each other. She thought it might change her life forever. And if that change meant she couldn't be friends with Maria anymore, well . . .

"All right. I'm going to draw something on this pad," Dr. Doyle said. "Then both of you will try to draw the same thing." He started sketching, his Magic Marker squeaking as he worked.

"All right, but no more dirty pictures, Doc," Michael said.

Cameron closed her eyes and tried to look like she was picking up some ESP vibe. It was hard not to smile. It was kind of sick how much she was actually enjoying being locked away down here.

With Michael. That was the key phrase—underlined and italicized.

Cameron heard the lab door swing open, and her eyes popped open. A guard walked in, bringing the room's guard total to three. "Sheriff Valenti wants to see you," the new guard told Cameron.

"Oooh. Someone's in trouble," Michael singsonged, trying to conceal his concern.

"Watch out for the doctor," she mouthed before she left the room, escorted by the guard. In silence, she followed him down the corridor.

The guard stopped in front of Valenti's office and

knocked once. "Enter," Valenti answered. The guard opened the door for Cameron, and she stepped inside. The guard shut the door behind her.

Cameron sat down in one of the chairs in front of the sheriff's desk without waiting for an invitation.

"The security camera showed you with a machine gun," Valenti said.

She kept silent for a few more seconds. "That's right," she finally replied. "You want Michael to trust me. Do you think he would trust someone who didn't back him up during the escape attempt?"

"So the machine gun was just for realism," Valenti said. Cameron couldn't tell if he was buying her story or not.

"Michael knows I'm not stupid," Cameron answered. "It would look pretty suspicious if I left a weapon on the floor when we were supposed to be fighting our way out of this place."

"I see your point," Valenti agreed, "but I also see that you're getting pretty tight with our buddy Michael. I see the looks you flash him. You're having a little too much fun. It's all right to have fun, gypsy girl, but you better come up with some info soon. And I expect advance warning if Michael comes up with another escape plan. All you have to do is pretend you're sick, and one of the guards will bring you to me."

"Whatever," Cameron said. "So is that it?"

"Pretty much," Valenti answered. "Has there been any problems with the parapsychological abilities cover story?"

"No, all the little tricks have been working fine."

"And you remember that if he touches you, he will learn a great deal about you, possibly including the fact that you have been sent to spy on him," Valenti said.

"Yeah, I remember." Cameron stood up and turned toward the door.

"Don't leave yet. I thought you might be interested in this," Valenti said.

Cameron turned around. Valenti was holding out a sheet of paper. Reluctantly she moved toward him, took it out of his hand, and flipped it over. Her hand was shaking.

Don't lose it in front of him, she ordered herself, but her hand wouldn't stop shaking. The paper fluttered to the floor. She glanced down at it and saw her own face staring back. The words *Have you seen this girl?* were printed in huge letters underneath. "It's nice to know how much your parents care, isn't it?" Valenti asked her. "They've plastered these posters over most of the state."

"I'm not going back there," Cameron said. Her voice was shaking, too.

"If you don't want to go back, you know what to do. Get me the names of the other aliens," he said. "But know this—I'm not willing to wait forever."

Cameron looked indignant, almost mad. "But he didn't even admit he was an alien until I said—"

"You're free to go," Valenti told her.

Free, yeah.

Cameron turned and walked out the door. She shut it quietly behind her. She'd shown Valenti way too much emotion already. Her hands were still trembling.

The guard led the way back to the lab. They got there way too fast. Cameron pulled in a deep breath as they headed inside. Michael gave her that killer grin of his the second he saw her, and a wave of hot nausea rushed through her.

It's not like I lied to him about everything, she thought. I did run away. Valenti did find me. And my parents do see me as a freak, even if it's not for the reason Michael thinks.

His friends, whoever they are, they have powers, like Michael, she reminded herself, trying to stop the sick feeling from building. Even if I give Valenti their names, it's not like he's just going to be able to go round them up. And if he does, if he does, at least they'll have each other.

I'm the only one looking out for me.

Look! Down in the dirt! It's a worm! It's a bug! No, it's Alex Manes . . . Understanding Guy!

Yep, that was him. Who else would have agreed to stake out the compound with Isabel only days after she'd shown him the door? Other guys would be cursing her name, poking out the eyes in every picture of her, telling their friends that she was evil spawn. But not our hero. Understanding Guy just sucked it up and said sure, if Isabel wanted him to spend ten or so hours crouched down behind some scratchy bushes in a little arroyo, he could do that. With a smile.

Alex took a swig out of his sports bottle. No matter how much water he drank, he felt like he was sweating out more.

"Uh, Alex, there's something I wanted to talk to you about," Isabel said. "You know the other day, when I said I didn't think we should see each other anymore?"

He nodded, although he didn't remember it quite that way. First, Isabel hadn't *said* anything, she'd shrieked. And what she'd shrieked had been, well, not quite so polite.

"Anyway, I just wanted you to know that it really didn't have anything to do with you," Isabel continued. "You were right about me being totally stressed about Michael and everything. And now there's Adam to deal with. It just seems like there's too much going on for me to be with anybody right now. Even someone as great as you."

This was definitely a job for Amazing Understanding Guy. Alex put on his best all-is-forgiven smile. He opened his mouth to say something that would make her feel totally okay for slamming him—but no words came out.

"I mean, if it was a different time in my life," Isabel said.

She kept talking, but Alex couldn't listen anymore.

He just did not need this. Sure, Isabel was beautiful. And when she touched him, instant meltdown. But she was totally selfish, spoiled, conceited, thoughtless—He stopped himself. He'd need his computer to do a really complete list.

"You know what, Isabel? You don't have to worry about it. The whole thing is fine with me," Alex told her. "In fact, it's great. You saved me the trouble of coming up with a nice way to break up with you."

"So, we're just going to break in?" Maria asked. Her feet felt like they'd taken root in the sidewalk across the street from Sheriff Valenti's house. She wasn't sure she'd ever be able to move from this spot.

"We probably won't have to do the breaking part," Liz answered. "I bet there's a door or a window open in back. At least there always is at my house."

"If we wait for Kyle, he'd probably just let us in," Maria said. "Having you in his house has to be one of his major fantasies."

"You don't think he'd find it kind of suspicious if I just came over to his house after telling him to stay away from me, like, four thousand times?" Liz asked. "Besides, he knows I'm with Max."

Maria smiled at her. "I don't think Kyle exactly thinks with his brain when you're around."

"Oh, gross." Liz scrunched up her face in disgust. "You have just given me a picture I really did not need to see," she complained. Then she pulled in a deep breath. "Are you ready?"

"I guess. Except for this problem I'm having with my feet. They won't actually move," Maria answered.

"We're doing this for Michael," Liz reminded her.

"Oh, that was low," Maria said as they started across the street.

"But effective," Liz shot back. "Let's just act like we've been invited and head straight through the back gate."

"Do you think Isabel will end up with Michael now that she and Alex are broken up?" Maria burst out as they crossed the Valentis' front lawn.

The question just popped out of her mouth. Maria had been wanting to ask Liz that for days. But she kept telling herself that was not what she should be thinking about. All she should be worried about was getting Michael free. Spending even a few seconds thinking about who he was going to go out with when he got home was just disgusting.

But she couldn't help it. Of course she wanted Michael home safe. Of course that was the most important thing. Of course she wanted that even if he ended up with Isabel.

Of course she would have to curl up in a little ball and die if he did.

Liz led the way through the gate and tried the side door. Locked. "You didn't answer my question," Maria said as they moved around the house to the glass door leading to the dining room.

"I didn't answer because I don't know," Liz replied as she gave the door a tug. It was locked, too. "I guess it could happen, but maybe it's better just to wait and see and not think about it too much beforehand. At least you told Michael how you felt about him, so however it goes down, you won't have to keep wondering if it would have turned out differently if he knew how you really felt."

Yeah, so when he chooses Isabel, I'll be positive that he knew I loved him and that he didn't care, Maria thought. That will make it way, way better.

Liz reached another sliding glass door, this one leading to the living room. She tried it, and it slid open soundlessly. "We're in," she told Maria.

Maria listened hard, but she didn't hear any footsteps. They'd been pretty sure the house was empty, and it seemed like they were right. "Let's move before my feet go on strike again," she said. She stepped into the living room, Liz right alongside her.

"If Valenti has an office here, it's probably down that hall," Liz said.

Maria nodded and took a right. The place is like a hotel, she thought as she glimpsed a bedroom through an open door. Totally impersonal. It was worse than a hotel, really. Hotels usually had some kind of bad painting on the wall. The walls here were bare.

The next door was closed. Maria opened it. Jackpot—desk, computer, filing cabinet.

"Files or computer?" Liz asked.

"Files," Maria answered. She hurried over to the low three-door cabinet and sat down in front of it. She pulled open the top drawer, and the whole thing almost toppled over on her. She used one hand to hold the cabinet in place and one hand to pull out the first file. It was all Kyle stuff. Report cards, a suspension notice, some vaccination records. Nothing useful.

The second file wasn't any better. Just canceled checks and old bills. The third file had tax stuff. The fourth file had Sheriff Valenti's birth certificate, the lease for the house, and a copy of his car registration.

"Valenti's middle name is Elmer. It's just not as easy to be scared of someone named Elmer," Maria said. She started to giggle.

"Oh no, Maria. Not now," Liz begged.

Maria locked her teeth together and tried to think of something completely unfunny, like that guy Carrot Top. But she heard something that made her giggle even harder, so hard she couldn't keep it in. It was the sound of a door opening.

Liz moved up behind her and wrapped her hand over Maria's mouth. Maria squeezed her eyes shut and took deep, slow breaths until she felt the urge for hysterical giggling fade. She reached up and pushed Liz's hand away.

"I think whoever it was headed to the kitchen," Liz whispered. "If we keep all the way to the right side of the hall, I think we can make it to the living room and out the door without being spotted."

Maria nodded her agreement. She stepped out of the office and pressed her back to the right wall. She crept sideways down the hallway, her eyes locked on her feet.

About halfway there, she coached herself. Keep moving. She took another step, then felt Liz's fingers dig into her arm. Maria looked up—and saw Kyle Valenti staring at them.

Maria's heart slammed up, lodging in her throat. She could feel it in there, a hot, meaty lump. At least it was saving her from another laugh attack.

"What the hell are you doing in here?" Kyle demanded.

"We're, uh, decorating all the football players' houses. You know, as a surprise to . . . give our guys a boost before the next game." Maria held up her crocheted bag, glad it was her biggest one. "We have crepe paper and everything. Rah, rah!"

Kyle crossed his arms over his chest. "I'm not on the football team," he informed her.

"Uh, uh, uh. . . " Maria swallowed hard, trying to shove her heart back into place.

"Really? This is all my fault!" Liz cried. "I always think of you as on the team. I guess because you're so big and strong. Well, we better go find the right house." She grabbed Maria by the arm and pulled her past Kyle. They raced out the front door and didn't stop running until they rounded the corner at the end of Kyle's block.

"Did you actually look at Kyle Valenti and say, 'You're so big and strong'?" Maria gasped.

"Sickening, isn't it?" Liz answered. "At least we got a look at Valenti's office."

"And found nothing." Maria sighed. "At least I didn't."

"Me neither," Liz said. "I hope the others are having more luck than we are."

Max shot a look at Adam. Was he cute? Max took another fast glance. It's not like he had to watch the road *that* carefully. It was straight, and flat, and pretty much empty, with the desert stretching out on both sides.

But no matter how often he took one of his fast peeks, Max just couldn't decide. Was Adam cute? Well, what he meant was, would girls think Adam was cute? It was a hard call. There were some things, like kittens or fuzzy ducklings, that were pretty much no-brainers. Definitely cute.

But Adam. Max was pretty clueless, although he had heard Maria saying that Adam's eyes were the most amazing shade of green. And eyes, they were important to girls, right?

Even if Maria thinks he's cute, that doesn't mean Liz thinks he's cute, Max told himself. And even if Liz *does* think he's cute, that doesn't mean anything. I mean, admit it, you think other girls besides Liz are cute. Like Maria. Be honest, you think Maria is walking, giggling cuteness.

But Liz. Whoa. Liz was so beautiful, it practically made him dizzy every time he saw her. She affected him the way no other girl ever did or ever would. And that's what he wanted Liz to feel about him. And that's most assuredly what he didn't want her to feel about Adam. Not like she did. Or at least he was pretty sure she didn't. But if Adam was cute, she might.

Wasn't there some study about how when a woman looked at a man and found him attractive, her pupils dilated? Maybe that's how he could tell if—

If Michael or Alex could hear what you're thinking, they would rag on you for the rest of your days, Max told himself.

"I guess we're far enough away from town for our practice session," Max said. He pulled the Jeep off the highway and drove another mile or so into the desert.

Adam was being awfully quiet. Max wondered what he'd been thinking about during the drive. Was he thinking about Liz? Was—

Max told himself to shut up and pulled the Jeep to a stop.

"Do you have a headache?" Adam asked. "You keep rubbing your head."

Max hadn't even realized he'd been doing it. It wasn't that he had a headache exactly, but there was this constant pressure behind his eyes. He thought it was from trying to block all the sensations and knowledge from the collective consciousness. It's not that he didn't want to learn everything he could about his heritage. But when he let himself experience the consciousness, it was all-consuming. And he couldn't afford the distraction right now. Later, after Michael was safe, there would be plenty of time to give himself over to it.

"I'm okay," he told Adam. "Any ideas on what we should try first? We're looking for anything that will give us more firepower when we break Michael out."

He didn't say "if." There was no "if" in this situation. In two days the group was going in, and Michael was coming out with them.

"Dr. Doyle, the guy who did most of the tests on me, had me try to explode things once," Adam said. "The biggest thing I ever managed was a grape. But together . . ."

"Let's try it. So when you blew up the grape, did you just push the molecules apart or what?" Max asked.

"I . . . I don't know," Adam answered. "I never really think about how I'm doing something—I just do it. Somehow it just comes out."

"Whoa. I've never experienced it like that," Max said, feeling a stab of envy. "Maybe it's because I've spent most of my life trying not to use any power if I didn't have to, and you grew up pushed to find out all the ways you could use yours."

"You didn't use your powers because you were afraid of scaring people, right?" Adam asked.

He's already figured out that's not the only reason, Max realized. Adam had been out of the compound for less than a week, and he'd already seen enough to teach him that humans, at least some humans, would want him dead if they knew the truth about him. Max could hear that knowledge in Adam's voice.

Adam was waiting for an answer.

"We don't use our powers in front of people partly because it would scare them. But also because when they do get scared, they can lash out. There are definitely people out there who would hurt you, Adam, just because you're different."

Adam nodded, his face somber. In that moment he looked like such a little boy. It was hard for Max to believe he'd actually been obsessing about whether Liz could possibly go for him.

"So what should we try and blow up?" Max asked. He and Adam would have to have a much longer discussion about humans later, but now they needed to get some training time in.

"Cactus?" Adam asked, nodding toward one about fifty feet away.

"Okay." Max reached out and touched Adam's arm. Instant connection. The only problem was, the images from Adam filled his vision. He couldn't even see the cactus.

Max tried to block the images, the way he'd been doing with the stuff from the collective consciousness.

The images from Adam slowed, then faded. Max stared at the cactus.

"Ready?" he heard Adam ask.

"One second," he answered. He still wasn't sure how to do this. Adam said he just *did* it, but Max needed a method.

Maybe you don't, he told himself. Just stop thinking so much.

"On three," he told Adam. He could feel something growing between him and Adam, a force being generated. "One. Two. Three."

Max let the force loose, trying to aim it at the cactus. A second later he felt something wet against his cheek. He reached up and pulled away a hunk of mushy cactus. It had exploded so fast, he hadn't even seen it happen. Lucky he didn't get hit by a spiny chunk.

"That was cool!" Adam cried.

"Yeah, that could come in very handy at the compound," Max answered.

Adam's happy smile faded. "Let's try something else," Max said quickly.

"One time Dr. Doyle wanted me to set something on fire with my power. We could work on that. I couldn't do it, but there were things I couldn't do by myself that I could do with Michael," Adam answered.

"I'll go put a ball of paper on the ground." Max started to get out of the Jeep.

"Why don't we try that rock over there?" Adam asked.

"A rock? Rocks aren't exactly flammable," Max said. "But sure, let's go for it." They could always try something easier later. Adam grabbed Max's wrist, starting the connection.

Max let the feeling of power build up until he could feel it practically screaming to get out. "Okay, on three. One, two, three." He set the power free, and an instant later the rock began to smoke.

Come on, come on, Max thought. He let more power build, preparing for a second blast.

Out of the corner of his eye he saw a little brown rabbit hop over to a piece of the cactus remains and take a nibble. Then it hopped toward the rock.

"Adam, be careful. We don't want to hit the—"

Max felt the power zing free. Then he heard the rabbit give a scream.

Max ripped his hand away from Adam. "Stop!" he shouted. "You're going to kill it!"

The rabbit's back legs jerked frantically, as if it were trying to run but couldn't. "No! Adam, look what you're doing! You've got to pull the power back!"

Max grabbed Adam by the shoulders and knocked him out of the Jeep, tackling him to the ground like an angry football player. Max glanced up and saw the rabbit bound away.

"Why the hell did you do that? Did you think it was fun? Did you think—"

"What?" Adam asked. He shoved himself to his feet and brushed some of the dirt off his jeans.

"What?" Max cried. "You're asking me what? You almost killed that helpless rabbit—"

"I did?" Adam cried. "I didn't mean—I didn't even know. I felt kind of . . . out of control."

Adam looked at the spot where the rabbit had been. Max had to admit, Adam looked genuinely devastated. But Max had seen his face when the rabbit had squealed.

Adam had been smiling.

Liz twisted her hair into a knot on the top of her head. She noticed Adam following her every movement with his eyes. She could almost feel his fingers on the places his eyes touched. Sliding up her neck. Twining in her hair. She wasn't sure how to react. One part of her was flattered at being so admired, but another part of her ached for privacy.

She scooted down the sofa and cuddled up closer to Max.

"Oh no. You guys aren't going to turn into one of that kind of couple, are you?" Maria whined.

"What kind of couple?" Liz asked.

"Let me just ask you a few questions," Maria answered. "Have you ever shared a piece of gum with Max—a piece of gum that you've already chewed for a while? Have you ever engaged in any kind of baby talk? Do you often hear shouts of 'get a room' when you're out in public? If you've answered yes to any of the above, it may already be too late. You may already be that kind of couple."

"Don't worry. We're not going there," Liz promised. "Are we, Maxie-waxie, my little googie face?"

"Where are Alex and Isabel?" Max asked. "I want to get this done."

"This" being coming up with the plan to rescue Michael. Which more than explained how distracted Max was.

"They're only a couple of minutes late. I'm sure they'll be here soon," Maria answered.

"How can you be sure of that?" Max snapped.

"I guess we can't. Hey, doesn't Isabel have a cell phone? I could call and see where they are," Liz volunteered.

"I'll do it," Max answered.

Before he could stand up, Liz heard the front door open. A moment later Alex and Isabel appeared. Isabel headed for the couch, and Alex perched on the edge of Maria's chair, putting them pretty much as far away from each other as they could get and still be sitting in the living room.

Spending time alone on the stakeout obviously hadn't led to any kiss-and-make-up action. Liz didn't know if that was good or bad. Isabel's personality always seemed completely opposite to Alex's, but sometimes that could actually work for people.

"We found nada," Alex announced, obviously eager to get down to business and then get out of there.

Max checked his watch. "Our parents could get home soon, and this isn't a conversation I want them walking in on. Maybe we should take turns keeping watch for them. Adam, do you mind doing the first one? You can see the driveway from the kitchen window."

"Okay." Adam stood up and headed out of the room. As he passed behind the couch, Liz felt a whisper-soft touch on her shoulder. Guess Adam needs a stronger hint, she thought.

As soon as Adam was gone, Isabel turned to her brother. "What's the deal? We both know Mom and Dad are at their office in Clovis. They won't be home for hours."

"Something happened when Adam and I practiced combining our powers," Max answered.

His tone jerked Liz out of her thoughts and pulled all her attention to him. Max almost sounded frightened. This wasn't about coming up with a plan to get Michael out. Something else was wrong. Something major.

"We were trying to set a rock on fire, and this rabbit hopped out," Max continued. "Adam was just about to *incinerate* the poor thing, until I tackled him. One second its nose was twitching, the next second it was squealing. I think he's got an evil side or something."

A small sound of distress escaped Maria's lips.

"Oh, man," Alex muttered.

No. The word exploded in Liz's brain.

"It had to be an accident," Isabel exclaimed. "The power slipped out of his control or something."

Max shook his head. "You weren't there. You didn't see it. The rabbit screamed. It sounded almost like a person, really loud and high. And Adam was smiling like he was watching a good show on TV or something."

"I can't believe Adam could do that," Maria said.

"We have no idea what he's capable of," Max answered, his voice flat. "We don't know what they did to him in that place. Maybe they've spent years turning him into some kind of killing machine."

"Max is right," Alex said. "We've only been around Adam a few days."

Liz got a flash of Adam spinning in her backyard, laughing as the grass tickled his bare feet. "Adam is about as far from a killing machine as you can get," she told them.

"Of course you'd say that," Max answered. She felt his body tighten, and he shifted away from her.

"Of course I'd say that because what?" Liz demanded. "Because Adam has a little crush on me? You really think that's why I'm defending him?"

"Yeah. I do," Max said bluntly.

"I'm glad to know you think so highly of me," Liz shot back. She wrapped her arms around her waist.

"Adam doesn't have a crush on me, and I agree

with Liz," Isabel cut in. "He's completely gentle and sweet."

Maria turned to Max. "Do you think he's dangerous to us?"

"That's the question we need to decide before we go into the compound," Alex said. "What do you think, Max? Do you think there's any chance he could turn on us?"

Michael paced around his cell. Sometimes only needing two hours of sleep a night totally sucked. In here, he wouldn't mind needing twenty.

Okay, maybe not twenty. Twenty would mean he slept way more than Cameron, and Michael wouldn't want to miss any Cameron time. He shot a quick look into her cell. All he could see was the top of her head as she lay on her cot. He liked her hair, which was kind of weird because he usually went for long hair on girls.

He also usually went for girls with a few more curves. Cameron was long, lean, and had more muscles, well, not more than he did, but she was definitely a hard body.

Don't go any farther in that direction, Michael told himself. It wasn't a good idea for boys who lived in glass cells to think about sex stuff too much.

He flopped down on his bed and stared up at the glass ceiling and the cement ceiling far above it.

He wondered how far underground they were. Sometimes the idea of being underground completely creeped him out. It was like being buried alive.

Michael jumped up, suddenly feeling way too much like he was lying in a coffin. He shot another glance over at Cameron. He would let himself look at her a little longer if the guards weren't around. He didn't like the feeling of having people out there going, "Look, Alien Boy wants the human girl."

Was that even true? Did he want Cameron? Oh, yeah.

Okay, harder question, Michael thought. Would you want Cameron if she wasn't the only girl in this place?

The answer came just as fast. Oh, yeah.

Even harder question. Do you want her more than you want Maria or Isabel?

Isabel, whoa. How did she get in that question? Isabel was practically like his sister. He didn't think of Isabel *that* way.

Except, remember that day you were wrestling over the remote? he asked himself. He'd gotten this flash of what it would be like to see her in the non-almost-like-a-sister category, and it had been . . . intense. Body-burning intense.

That explained how Isabel got into the question. Michael shoved his hands through his hair. He'd really been trying not to think about Maria down here. He had enough to deal with without trying to decide how he felt about Maria saying she loved him.

The *love* word. It pretty much freaked him out. It felt too monumental. Maybe it didn't feel that way to people who had real families. Max and Liz had their parents saying "I love you" practically all the time. So it's like they'd had the chance to get used to hearing the words. Michael hadn't.

Okay, here's another question, he thought. Do you *love* any of them?

Isabel. He definitely loved Isabel, not that he'd ever actually told her that.

Stop right there, he ordered himself. You know we're not talking about an I-love-you-like-a-sister kind of thing. Or the you're-a-great-friend-and-I-love-you kind of thing. So what's your answer? Do you love Maria, Cameron, or Isabel?

Liz flipped her pillow over and pressed her face into the cool side. Why wasn't she asleep? She needed to be asleep.

Tomorrow they were going into the compound, and she couldn't be all fuzzy and out of it.

Well, she could be. She could also be dead if she screwed up.

Oh, there's a thought that would put her right to sleep. Liz decided that as long as her brain was spinning, she'd give it something to focus on. It was periodic chart time. Going over the chart in her mind always calmed her down. She'd do the rare earth elements first.

There was yttrium, symbol Y, atomic number 39, atomic weight 88.9059. It wasn't always classified as a rare earth element. Sometimes it was classified as a transition—

A soft sound from the backyard grabbed Liz's attention. Was Adam moving around down there? She swung herself out of bed and hurried over to the window—just in time to see Adam slipping back into the shed.

Where had he been? Liz pulled on her robe and headed to the back door even while she was telling herself he probably just had to pee or something. She slid open the door, crept over to the shed, and gave a little knock. Adam answered instantly, a huge smile spreading across his face when he saw her.

Oops, Liz thought. By visiting him in the middle of the night, I have now probably destroyed any of the I'm-with-Max hints that did manage to make it into his head.

"Hey, I heard you come back in," she said. "I just wanted to see if you were okay. Is there something you needed? Are you too cold out here or anything?"

"Everything's good," Adam answered. "Do you

want to come in for a minute? I could make toast."

Liz smiled. She had gotten him a toaster as sort of a housewarming present. How could a guy whose biggest love in life is making toast be dangerous? she thought. Max has to be wrong about what happened out in the desert. Killing the rabbit had to be an accident.

"I better not. My parents will freak if they notice I'm gone," Liz answered. She turned toward the house, hesitated, and turned back to Adam. "So where'd you go?" she asked.

"Huh?" Adam asked.

"You went out. I just wondered where you went," Liz said.

Adam scrunched his eyebrows together. "Where I went," he repeated softly. "I don't think I went anywhere."

"I'm not mad or anything," Liz assured him. "Although you do need to be careful. I was just curious because, like I said, I saw you coming back home."

Adam stiffened up. "I just went to the minimart for some butter to put on my toast," he answered in a rush.

It made sense. But there was something about the way he said it that made Liz think he was lying. Why? What was he doing in the middle of the night that he needed to lie about?

Liz thought about asking to see the butter, but

that seemed way too stupid. And if Adam was lying for some reason, maybe it was better to let him think she believed him. Better and safer.

"Are you sure you don't want me to make you some?" He smiled at her, his lips stretching up over his teeth.

Liz shivered, and involuntarily she took a step away. Max and Alex were right. She didn't know Adam that well.

Adam carried a piece of toast with him to the Jeep. He ate it as he and the others headed out of town. Even though melted butter had seeped into every inch of the bread, the toast tasted dry, scratchy against his mouth and throat.

He was going back to the compound. He was going back to the place without sun. Without grass. Without anything that was real. And yet a part of him was looking forward to it. He was, technically, going home.

"Should we go over the plan again?" Alex asked.

"Please, can we not?" Maria answered. "The more we talk about it, the more I realize there's not much plan in our plan."

"Maybe we should see if we can come up with something better," Liz suggested.

"We already know we can't," Isabel said sharply. "We've gone over every possibility a million times."

Adam didn't say anything. It didn't matter to him one way or the other. He didn't need a plan to know what needed to be done in the compound.

"Isabel's right," Max said. "Let's just use the drive to get focused."

Adam leaned his head against the roll bar and tried to take in every detail about the town as they drove through. If things went wrong, he wanted a lot of real things to remember.

Then he realized that wasn't true. He didn't need a lot of things. He needed one thing. If he ended up locked in the compound again, he wanted to be able to remember every single detail of Liz's face. He turned and studied her, trying to memorize the curve of her upper lip, the exact color of her eyes, the way her hair tumbled alongside her cheek. He stared at her until he was sure he'd never forget even one of her eyelashes, then he closed his eyes.

Max said they should get focused, and he was right. Adam tried to picture himself walking into the compound, feeling unafraid.

Will I see . . . Daddy? The thought slammed through his brain.

Sheriff Valenti, Adam told himself. He isn't your father. He's nothing to you. You cannot let him stop you from doing what you need to do. You can't let anything stop you.

"You want to finish our game of truth or dare, Mickey?" Cameron asked.

Today's the day, she promised herself. Today is

the day I get the names Valenti wants and get out of here. Pretending to be Michael's friend while she was getting ready to screw him over was eating her guts out. She had to cut to the chase.

"How do you know when you've finished a game, anyway?" Michael asked. "There are no points. No one wins or anything."

"Someone loses, though," Cameron answered. "Every game of truth or dare I've ever played, someone breaks down crying. And that pretty much ends the game."

"Brutal," Michael said.

You don't know the half of it.

"Okay, it was my turn," Cameron said. "How did you know you were an alien? Truth or dare."

There, that should get this going in the right direction. Unless Michael chose a dare. Maybe this whole truth-or-dare ploy was a mistake.

"Basically I just started realizing I could do things that most people around me couldn't," Michael answered. "Then later I saw pictures of some pieces of metal found around the crash site after the Roswell Incident. The symbols on them matched a few of the symbols from my incubation pod, so that's how I started figuring out the truth."

"So the Roswell Incident really happened?" Cameron asked. "I thought it was just a way for the town to sell a bunch of T-shirts and, you know, alien piñatas."

I can't believe we're sitting here talking about the Roswell Incident. This whole thing has got to be a joke, she thought. Or some kind of weird test.

Yeah, that made sense, actually. Maybe Michael was an actor, and Valenti and that doctor were monitoring her reactions to him, trying to see if she'd really accept what Michael told her as real.

A test. Of course. That had to be it. Cameron felt herself relax a little. If this was all just a test, then it didn't matter if she gave Valenti the information he wanted once she managed to get it. It's not like he'd round up a bunch of Michael's actor friends and throw them in the compound. No, they'd just bring in the next test subject, and Michael would go through his whole act again while Valenti and the doctor made notes.

"It really happened," Michael answered.

"So, are you really, like, more than fifty years old?" she asked. Let's see how you answer that, actor boy, she thought.

"What, you don't like older guys?" Michael asked, then he shoved his fingers through his spiky black hair. "I actually didn't break out of my pod until about ten years ago. I looked like I was about a seven-year-old kid. So, you tell me how old I am."

He's not lying, Cameron thought.

You wanted him to be lying, so you told yourself he was, she thought. That way you wouldn't have to think about your own lies.

140

"It's your turn," she told Michael. She had to keep the game moving so she could find out what she needed to know. If she didn't do it fast, she wasn't sure she'd end up being able to do it at all.

"The other day, you knew I was going to kiss you and you pulled away. Why? Truth or dare," Michael said, his gray eyes intense.

"Truth," Cameron answered. "I know if you touch people, you can read their thoughts, and I didn't want you to read mine."

"It's not thoughts, exactly—more like pictures, pieces of memories," Michael answered. "And I wouldn't have."

"It doesn't just happen automatically?" Cameron asked.

"Nope. Does yours?"

"Mine?" Cameron forgot for a second she was supposed to have telepathic powers. "No, uh, I have to decide to use my juice."

"So is that the only reason you pulled away?" Michael asked.

If I say yes, he's going to want to kiss me, Cameron thought. And if he kissed her, she didn't know if she'd be able to finish her little spying assignment.

So say no, she told herself. Say that there's another reason you pulled away. Say you have a boyfriend. Say you have a headache. Say *something*.

"Yes," Cameron said.

Michael leaned toward her. You can still stop this, Cameron thought. Just pull away again. Kissing him is the worst-possible thing you could do.

She reached out, ran her fingers through his hair, and gently pulled his mouth down to hers. And for a long moment she forgot everything but the taste of him.

Then she pulled away. This was it. This was the moment where he was going to be the most open. She could feel it.

"I never thought anyone who knew what a total freak I am would want to kiss me," she said. She wasn't even going to have to ask him anything directly. He was going to tell her everything all on his own.

"You've never met anyone else who's . . . like you?" Michael asked.

"No," Cameron answered. Her stomach twisted itself into a knot. She ignored the pain.

"I had it so much easier than you did," Michael said.

Bring it to me, Cameron thought.

"I had Max and Isabel. They're . . . like me," he continued. "Their parents aren't. They don't know the truth at all. But the Evanses are great. They even call me their other son."

Game over. Those were the names she needed. Cameron's stomach cramped again.

"Are you okay?" Michael asked.

"No . . . no," Cameron said slowly. She added, "Actually, I'm sort of nauseous," she answered. "I'm going to see if the guard can get me some antacid or something."

Cameron shoved herself to her feet and knocked on the door. "I'm feeling sort of sick," she told the guard who opened it.

"Come with me," he said.

"We'll finish our game later when you're feeling better," Michael called.

"Okay," she answered, without looking back. She didn't want a last look. She had plenty to torture herself with already. She kept her eyes locked on the guard's back as he marched her to Valenti's office.

"I want five thousand dollars, and I want you to tell my parents that I'm heading to New York," Cameron announced the second she sat down in the chair across from Valenti's desk. She didn't want to give herself any time for second thoughts.

"While you'll be trotting off to California, I suppose," Valenti answered.

Cameron didn't answer. Valenti seemed to remember he'd lost their last round of the silence game. "I'll give you twenty-five hundred dollars," he said. "And no more. As soon as you give me the names."

"The other aliens are Max and Isabel Evans."

Max handed the binoculars to Adam. "There's the surveillance camera. See, it's in that crack at the top of the rock formation."

Adam nodded. He felt as if his body was freezing from the inside out, the coldness paralyzing more and more area with each moment.

"All we need to do is crack the glass," Max said. He grabbed Adam's wrist. Adam could hardly feel the pressure of Max's fingers. If their plan worked, in a few minutes he would be back inside the compound.

And in less than an hour you'll be back out, Adam reminded himself. The coldness invaded his heart. He knew there was no way it had stopped beating, but he couldn't feel it anymore.

"Everyone, get ready to run," Max ordered. He turned to Adam. "On three."

Adam kept the binoculars up so he could focus on the camera. He didn't need to see it, but it helped.

"One, two, *three.*"

Adam took the power that had been growing

since he and Max connected and hurled it out, out, out. Was it strong enough to make it all the way to the camera lens? He heard a soft popping sound, and the camera exploded into metal and glass confetti.

"Run!" Max yelled.

"Nice shooting, Tex," Alex called from behind Adam as they all raced toward the rock formation that hid the opening to the compound. Adam smiled. Or at least he thought he was smiling. He couldn't quite feel his lips anymore.

When he was about a hundred feet away from the formation, Adam slammed to a stop. He watched the others run past him and take up their positions. Then he waited. If Max was right, in a few minutes a couple of guards would come out to check on the camera.

This could be my last minute in the sun, Adam thought. But he couldn't feel the warmth. Even the New Mexico sun wasn't strong enough to penetrate his cold skin.

Come on. Come and get me, Adam thought. Just standing here, passively waiting to be led back into his prison, was the hardest part of the plan.

It shouldn't take them too long. It had only been a week since Michael and Isabel had broken into the compound. The guards would still be extra alert.

Adam heard a low humming sound, and the rock

formation slid apart in one smooth motion. It was time. He waited until he could see the guards moving toward the opening, then he ran toward them.

"Stay where you are!" one of the guards barked.

"I want to come back!" Adam cried. "I want to see my father!"

"We're coming out to get you," the other guard called. Adam noticed that she had her hand on her electric prod.

"Okay. Hurry! I'm scared!" Was that too much? Adam thought as the guards hesitated.

No, they were moving toward him. Side by side, they stepped through the opening in the rock formation. And Max and Isabel attacked. The guards never saw it coming. They fell to the ground, unconscious.

Adam raced up to them. "Help me move this one inside," Alex said. Adam hoisted the guard's legs and Alex grabbed her shoulders, then they carried her into the massive elevator just beyond the entrance.

Alex knelt down and quickly bound the guards' hands and feet with duct tape. He slapped a couple pieces of the tape on their mouths. "I love this stuff. You can use it on anything," he said.

"They can breathe and everything, right?" Maria asked, staring from Alex and Adam's guard to the guard Max and Isabel had just finished restraining.

"They'll be fine," Max reassured her. He hit the elevator button, and they started down.

Adam slid his hands under his armpits, trying to warm up his hands. How deep underground were they already? Ten feet? More?

The elevator continued its smooth descent. Finally it came to a stop with a tiny bump. The doors slid open.

Adam heard pounding feet. He scanned the small parking lot and saw a guard running away.

"We've been spotted," Max cried. "He's going to sound an alarm!"

They were here. Michael could feel them. Isabel, Max, and Adam. Coming to the rescue.

What were they, insane?

Michael sprang up from his cot and started to pace. They needed him. Something had already gone wrong. He'd just gotten a jolt of fear from all three of them.

He shot a glance at the two guards outside his cell. They clearly had no clue anything unusual was happening in the compound. At least not yet. That was something.

Michael took another lap in the small space to the right of his cot. He wished Cameron would get back. He didn't like the idea of her being out in the corridors right now, even with her guard escort. It would be way too easy for her to get caught in some kind of crossfire situation.

And he wouldn't be able to do anything about

it, sitting in this cell. He wasn't exactly going to be able to back up Max and the others from here, either.

His eyes flicked back and forth between the two guards. Was there some way he could take them both out?

You decided your first day in here that there was no way to handle two guards at once, he reminded himself. Don't do anything stupid, or your friends are only going to have a corpse to rescue.

"I'll get the guard. You go on," Isabel exclaimed.

She took off across the parking lot. She heard feet pounding behind her and threw a quick glance over her shoulder. Alex. Good. She might need some kind of backup.

The guard had to hear them, but he didn't turn. He kept running, veering off onto a long corridor. What was he doing? Why wasn't he trying to stop them?

Suddenly Isabel knew why. She spotted an intercom on the wall. The wall about six feet from the guard.

She pushed herself to run even faster.

Too late. The guard reached the intercom. "I have a situation here," he barked. "There—"

Alex shoved past Isabel and hurled himself at the guard's knees. They both went down.

Isabel reached them a second later. She saw the guard go for his prod. Without hesitation she slammed her foot down on his wrist. She heard a bone crack, and the prod rolled out of the guard's hand.

An instant later she heard the guard's machine gun clatter down the corridor. Knew Alex would be a good guy to have around, she thought. She threw herself down on her knees and pressed her fingers against the guard's forehead. Yeah, he was unarmed. But that didn't mean he wasn't dangerous.

She pulled in a few deep breaths and made the connection. Images flashed through her brain. A boy proudly displaying his hall monitor badge. A parrot in an enormous cage. The boy at an even younger age screaming as a clown handed him a purple flower.

Isabel heard a second heartbeat join hers. She was in. Now she just needed to find a good vein in his head. *Their* head. She chose a medium-sized one near the brain stem and concentrated. She could feel the pain she caused him. God, she hated doing this.

The connection broke. The guard had lost consciousness. Alex tossed her a roll of tape, and Isabel started to restrain the man. She froze as she heard the intercom crackle. "What kind of situation?" a voice demanded.

"Keep going," Alex said. "I've got it." He pushed down the intercom button. "There was some kind of power surge down here. One of the surveillance cameras went down for a few minutes, but it's back up. I'll do the report."

"Valenti will want a copy," the voice answered. "Make sure he gets it today."

"Roger that," Alex said.

"Roger that. Your dad would be so proud." Isabel slid a piece of tape over the guard's mouth and shoved herself to her feet.

"You okay?" Alex asked her.

"Yeah," she answered. "I want to keep going this way. I started feeling Michael a little more strongly once we turned down this corridor."

"Adam knows where Michael's being held," Alex reminded her.

"But this feels like the right way. Maybe they moved him after Adam escaped," Isabel answered.

"Let's check it out, then," Alex said. They started down the corridor.

"Thanks for coming with me," Isabel mumbled, without looking at him. Now that they weren't fighting for their lives, it felt a little strange to be paired up yet again.

"No problem," Alex answered.

Isabel tried to zero in on exactly where the feelings from Michael were concentrated. "I think he's somewhere to the left of us," she said. The corridor continued on in the same direction as far as she could see. But there was a door on the left a few feet away. Isabel didn't think Michael was that close. But maybe if they cut through that room, they'd find another passageway.

She rushed up to the door. It was one of those massive metal ones she remembered from the last time she was in the compound. She focused on the molecules and gave them a shove. The door squealed open.

"I know it's old-fashioned, but I always appreciate having a door opened for me," Alex said as he stepped through.

Isabel followed him, and her breath caught in her chest. It was like walking into one of her nightmares. There's a door on the other side of the room, she told herself. All you have to do is walk over to it. Don't look at anything. Just move.

She kept her eyes locked on the door. But she couldn't help catching glimpses of things. Scalpels, and scissors, and even a little saw.

You're halfway through, she thought. And it's not like any of this stuff is going to jump up and start dissecting you all by itself.

Another step. Then another. Then another. You can do it. She bumped into something hard and cold. She glanced down and immediately wished she hadn't. It was a high metal table with troughs lining two of the sides. To catch the blood, she realized.

She reached out and touched the back of Alex's shirt. She didn't want to grab onto him like some pathetic thing. She just wanted to keep two fingers on his shirt. That's all.

She couldn't stop a long, shaky sigh of relief from escaping as Alex reached for the door handle. But before he could pull the door open, Isabel felt a sharp pain in the back of her neck. She reached behind her and felt something sticking out of her skin. She yanked it free. A syringe.

She turned and saw a man in a white lab coat. "Where did you come—"

Her body gave a violent jerk, then her legs started to spasm. The drain in the tile floor filled her vision as she fell.

"That's the door to Michael's cell," Adam whispered.

"Are there guards inside?" Max asked.

Adam shook his head. "They're usually out here."

If they were usually out there, then why did Adam lead them down this corridor without any warning?

Do you think there's any chance he could turn on us? That question of Alex's had been running through Max's head all day, like some kind of Muzak from hell.

Max just didn't know. Maybe they should have

left Adam at home. But Max thought that he might need the extra power.

This is not the time to start rethinking your decision, he told himself. Adam's here now. There's no turning back.

"You two keep watch," he said to Liz and Maria. "If you see guards, try and knock on the cell door or give us some kind of signal."

"We'll kick their butts if they come near us," Maria answered, her voice quaking.

"Go," Liz urged.

"Let's connect here in case we need to use our combined power inside," Max said. Adam reached out and grabbed him by the wrist.

Do you think there's any chance he could turn on us?

Max tried to ignore that question as he and Adam crept up to the cell door. Adam reached out with his free hand and swung it open.

Wait. There was something wrong. Shouldn't it have been locked?

Before Max could formulate any kind of answer for himself, Adam stepped through the door, pulling Max with him.

"Max Evans. You've saved me the trouble of coming to pick you up."

Max jerked his head toward the voice and saw Sheriff Valenti sitting behind a wide desk. A girl with short red hair sat in one of the chairs across from it.

Adam had led him right to the sheriff's office. He'd clearly been planning this all along. But why?

"I hope your sister is here, too. Not that it would be too difficult to run into town and get her," Valenti said. "In fact, I'd enjoy it. I've spent half my life looking for the two of you. Soon I'll have all my aliens safely tucked into their beds."

Max couldn't answer. He felt a twisting in his gut. Valenti knew the truth.

Max grabbed Adam's hand and made the connection.

"Won't that be nice, Adam?" Valenti asked in a hideous kindergarten voice. "You always wanted a bigger family than just you and Daddy."

Max felt the power begin to grow inside him, doubling in size every second. Adam's getting ready to use it, he realized.

Maybe we could make a circle of fire around Valenti to trap him, Max thought. Or maybe with our combined power we can knock him out from here without touching him to make a connection.

Max turned toward Adam. Maybe he could signal him to—

His heart froze. Adam was smiling at Valenti. The same smile he'd given the rabbit.

"Adam, no!" Max yelled. He tried to jerk his hand away, but Adam's fingers were digging into his flesh.

Max twisted around and slammed his fist into

Adam's side. Adam released him. "I don't need you, anyway," he muttered.

A flash of brilliant white light filled the room, reflecting off the walls, blinding Max. He blinked hard, trying to clear his vision. He thought he saw Valenti sitting behind his desk. But that was impossible. There was no way he could have survived.

Max wiped his running eyes with his sleeve and took a step closer to the desk. Valenti *was* sitting there, coated entirely in ash, not one speck of skin showing. He was absolutely motionless. What had Adam done to him?

He heard the girl in the chair behind him making these low moaning sounds deep in her throat. He knew he should go to her, but he couldn't stop staring at Valenti.

Adam moved up next to Max. He leaned forward, pursed his lips, and blew. With a soft whispering sound, Valenti crumbled into a pile of dust.

"Why did you do that?" Max shouted. "There were other ways we could have dealt with him. We never use our power to kill. Never!"

Adam didn't respond.

Max felt a trace of power in the room. It was building fast.

Do you think there's any chance he could turn on us?

Max whipped his head toward Adam. Adam smiled at him.

"What the hell did you do to her?" Alex screamed at the doctor.

Isabel gave another jerk, her eyes wide and staring. Alex could practically feel the pain in his own body.

The doctor dropped to his knees next to her. "I didn't mean to hurt her. I just gave her a shot of a fast-acting tranquilizer. It shouldn't have caused this reaction. I only wanted to detain you until I could call Valenti or one of the guards."

Alex reached down and yanked the doctor to his feet. He wrapped his arm around the man's neck to hold him still. Then he searched the pockets of the doctor's lab coat, coming up with two more syringes. He threw them across the room.

"I'm going to let you go now," Alex said into the doctor's ear. "And here's what you're going to do—you're going to do whatever it takes to save her life. She dies, and I do to your head what I did to that door." Alex used his free hand to point to the metal door Isabel had crushed open, then he shoved the doctor away.

"I may need to draw some blood to find out why she's having this reaction," the doctor answered, his words tumbling out on top of each other.

"Fine. Stay in sight. And if you think about doing anything stupid, I want you to look at the door and think again," Alex snapped. He sat down next to Isabel and took her hand in his. At least she'd stopped spasming.

He reached out with his free hand and brushed her hair away from her forehead. He felt something wet under his fingers. Did she cut herself when she fell? Alex leaned close. "Get over here and tell me what this is," he ordered the doctor.

The doctor rushed to Alex's side and crouched down next to him. "It looks like some kind of primitive gill," he said.

"A gill?" Alex exploded.

"This happened to Adam once when he had a high fever," the doctor answered. "I don't know how much you know about your own physiology, but your body is designed to adapt to whatever environment it is in."

My physiology? Alex thought. Then he realized the doctor must think he was an alien, too, since Alex had taken credit for the door.

"Occasionally it can malfunction and adapt when it isn't necessary," the doctor continued. "Look, the gill is closing already."

Alex moved his gaze to Isabel's forehead just in time to see her skin smooth itself back into place.

"I think it will be safer if we just let this run its course," the doctor said. "I don't think it will take long. If I'd realized the tranquilizer could cause this reaction . . ." He let the sentence trail off.

"You're going to be okay, Isabel," Alex promised.

"I'm right here with you. I'm going to be here the whole time." Alex felt her hand move in his. "Yeah, see, I'm here." He squeezed her hand back. Her fingers felt . . . different. Alex opened his hand so he could see hers.

Her fingers had always been long and slender, but now they were almost twice as long and as thin as pencils. As Alex watched, one finger was absorbed into the side of her hand.

His breath started coming in harsh pants. Maintain, he ordered himself. This is just Isabel. He closed his hand around hers again and turned back toward her face.

He didn't recognize her. There was nothing that remained of the Isabel he knew. Her head was huge. So were her eyes. And they were completely black.

Alex took the Isabel creature in his arms and began to run toward what he hoped was an exit. Then—in an instant so quick that it seemed like a hallucination—Isabel morphed back into Isabel again.

"Put me down, you big goon," Isabel said, smiling.

Alex set her down. Looking her straight in the eyes, he said, "We've got to get out of here, Izzy." Taking her cue, Isabel grabbed his hand and ran.

Michael had to get out of this cell. Now. Isabel needed him. He'd felt a blast of pain from her that had practically knocked him to the floor.

159

But Hubba and Bubba, his guards, were still out there. Still two of them. Still one of him. Right now they were sitting in a couple of chairs, facing Cameron's cell. They spent much more time with their eyes on her than on him, for obvious reasons, and they hadn't bothered to flip the chairs back around in his direction.

There's got to be a way to do this, Michael thought. If I surprise them, maybe I can manage to take them both out. Only there was this thing about glass cells. They made it hard to arrange any kind of surprise.

But he had to try. And he could think of only one possible way. He walked over to the wall behind the two guards and leaned on it with his hands pressed against the glass to either side of his waist.

Hubba—or Bubba, he still hadn't decided which was which—turned around. "Miss your girl-friend?" he mouthed.

Michael gave what he hoped was a sheepish grin and stared longingly toward Cameron's empty cell. Hubba—or Bubba—turned back around, and Michael focused his attention on the molecules of glass beneath his hands. He nudged them apart gently, taking his time.

This actually might work, he thought as a hole began to open up underneath both of his hands. It would definitely work if Cameron was over in her cell. Then there would be no chance these two would notice what he was doing.

Where was she, anyway? She didn't seem *that* sick. Could she and her guard escort have gotten captured by Max and the others? At least Adam knew Cameron, so he could tell everyone that she was on their side.

Michael gave the molecules a few more nudges, and he had his holes. Time to rock and roll. He shoved his hands through and grabbed Hubba and Bubba by the backs of their big necks.

Now would be a good time to connect, he told himself as he felt them turning toward him. He squeezed his eyes shut so he wouldn't be distracted by anything they were doing—and the images flooded his brain. He didn't know which came from who, and it didn't matter. He heard two heartbeats join his. That meant he'd have a lot of nice veins to choose from. He selected a good fat one from each head and squeezed. He opened his eyes in time to see the guards slump in their chairs, their heads touching.

"Don't they look sweet asleep like that," he muttered as he blasted a hole in the cell and stepped through. Time to find Isabel.

"Get out of here," Max ordered the red-haired girl. She didn't need to be told twice. She bolted.

The feel of power in the room was growing

stronger. Adam was clearly about ready to send Max off to heaven with Valenti.

But I'm not like Valenti, Max thought. Adam's not the only one who can use power. He focused on his own power, letting it build inside him.

It's gathering too slowly, he realized. I'm never going to be ready before Adam makes his move.

Max could run, but what good would that do? Adam would be right behind him, and out in the corridor Liz, Maria, and the girl would be in the line of fire.

Think. Be logical, Max ordered himself. You don't need the same amount of power as Adam. You just need enough to knock his power off course. And you already have that.

He did. He could feel it. But he had to use it at exactly the right moment. Too soon or too late, and he was dust.

"Come on, Max. Aren't you even going to try to save yourself?" Adam asked. "You could probably stub my toe with that little ball of power I *know* you've got over there."

"I told you, I don't use my power to hurt," Max answered. His so-called plan would only work if he just stood there and let Adam fire on him.

Adam shrugged. "Have it your way."

Max felt the power in the room pulse. Not yet, he told himself. Not yet. Then a blast of heat scorched his face.

Now! He focused his ball of power straight out in front of him, willing it through the air. A second later an explosion rocked the room, and the wall behind Max burst into flame.

"I can't stay," Adam said. "I have to spread my love around." He turned toward the door. When he opened it, it began to smoke.

Max reached the door only a few steps after Adam. By then orange flames covered it from top to bottom. He ducked through and saw Adam racing down the corridor with one hand outstretched, brushing against the wall. A trail of fire followed his fingers.

"He's burning the place down!" Maria cried.

"We've got to stop him. Come on!" Liz shouted.

Max grabbed her by the elbow. "He's too strong for us to fight," Max answered. "We've got to get Michael, find Isabel and Alex, and then get out of here while we still can."

"I know where he is," the red-haired girl exclaimed. She took off down the flaming corridor, Max, Liz, and Maria right behind her.

When the corridor branched, the girl went left with no hesitation. At least she seems like she really knows where she's going, Max thought.

Adam had obviously gone left, too. He must have been zigzagging because the walls on both sides were blazing. In places the flames were meeting in the ceiling, forming an arch of fire. And smoke. Max was dragging smoke into his lungs with every breath.

"It's right through this door down here," the girl shouted, her voice husky. She took another left. Immediately the air felt cooler. The fire was spreading in this direction, but slowly.

When they reached the metal door, Max focused on the molecules and slammed them. The door lurched open, and long fingers of flame shot through the opening. Max smelled the scent of his own singed hair as he backed away.

"Where is Michael's cell?" Maria cried.

"You can usually see it from here," the girl answered.

"Is there another way in?" Max asked. "I don't think we can make it through here." Even from a few feet away, the heat was almost unbearable. Max felt as if he were breathing lava instead of air. His throat and lungs and the lining of his nose were getting cooked.

"We'd have to double back and make a circle," the girl answered.

"We don't have time," Liz yelled.

"I'm going through," Maria announced. She pulled off her jacket and wrapped it around her head, then she plunged through the wall of flames.

"I guess it's now or never," Max said. He turned around, grabbed Liz by the back of the head, and planted a firm kiss on her surprised lips. "I love you," he said, looking her in the eyes. Before she could respond, he turned and ran.

Liz was so close behind him that she crashed into him when he came to a stop next to Maria. The red-haired girl was through a second later.

"Everybody okay?" Max asked, running his eyes around the group. He hadn't really registered any pain until he saw the blistered patches on Maria's face and realized pieces of his own skin felt as if they'd been splashed with oil from a french fry cooker.

"I don't see Michael," Maria cried. "All the cells are empty."

"That's his right there. Third one down. They must have taken him out," the girl said.

"Michael!" Max shouted. "Can you hear me? It's Max."

Maria started to yell, too. Liz and the girl joined in.

There was no answer.

"We're going to have to assume he got out of here somehow. Isabel and Alex, too," Max said. If he was wrong, he was leaving his sister and two of his best friends to certain death. But if he was right and they stayed down here continuing the search, he, Liz, Maria, and the girl would probably cook.

The girl nodded. "Let me take you on a tour. Starting with the exit."

"We can't leave them here," Maria protested.

"Anyone who stays is going to die," Liz told her, echoing Max's thoughts, as she often did. "They all know that. Michael, Alex, Isabel, and Adam—"

"Wait, did you hear that?" Max interrupted. He closed his eyes so he could listen better. No, he wasn't delusional. That was Michael. Wait. Michael and Alex.

"This way," the girl yelled. She took off down the row of glass cells. One exploded behind them, sending a rain of glass tinkling on the cement floor.

Now Max could hear Isabel, too. Her voice sounded totally different, all thick with smoke. He glanced toward the sound, and through the glass walls of one of the cells, he saw them. His heart expanded with relief.

"Let's go!" Michael shouted as the two groups converged. He wheeled to the left, leading the way. Max dropped to the back. He didn't want to get out and then find out someone had fainted from smoke inhalation on the way there.

"It's not that far," Michael called back as they ran. Max didn't know how he could tell. The smoke had turned the air into a thick gray blanket. With each breath it felt like less oxygen was making its way into his body.

Max's head started to spin. He couldn't feel his feet hitting the floor anymore. But they had to be. Because he was moving. Wasn't he? How could he tell? Everything just looked gray.

He felt an arm slip around him. "You stayed back

here to make sure everyone else got out, right?" he heard Liz ask. He could hardly see her. "You're just lucky you have me to look out for you."

"I got the door open," Michael yelled, his words mixed with a coughing fit.

The smoke got a little thinner, and Max pulled in a breath that felt like it was at least half air. A few moments later he and Liz were out.

"Keep moving," Alex commanded. "We're—"

Before he could finish, an explosion threw Max into the air. He landed hard on his back and saw an orange mushroom cloud shoot upward with a blinding flash of light.

Max slowly pushed himself to his feet, wheezing with every breath. What he saw when he looked toward the compound almost made him stop breathing altogether—the sand was burning. Low blue flames covered the ground in a huge square over the area where the compound lay.

Liz was immediately by Max's side, touching his face, her cheeks reddened from the heat. "I love you, too," she said, and smiled. He smiled back, then pulled her tight against his chest. She listened to his pounding heart for a moment, then turned back toward the flames.

The crew was watching in silence as the flames flickered and slowly died, leaving the sand black.

"Valenti's dead," he said finally. "Adam killed

him." He turned to his sister. "No more nightmares." She smiled at him, a tiny smile that didn't quite reach her eyes.

"Look!" Alex cried. "Look who else made it out!"

"No one could have survived that," Liz whispered. "It's impossible—"

Max followed Alex's gaze. A human form was emerging from the flames. Liz smiled, realizing she was wrong. It wasn't impossible.

It was Adam.

ROSWELL HIGH

SOME SECRETS ARE TOO DANGEROUS TO KNOW...

Don't miss Roswell High #6
The Stowaway

Michael is still having flashbacks of his escape from the underground compound. Only Cameron, the mysterious girl he met behind bars, seems to understand him — and realize that the sheriff may be gone but an even more dangerous enemy is out there ...

Cameron has fallen for Michael while in the compound ... spying on him for Sheriff Valenti. Now she feels guilty, and wishes she could tell him the truth. But how can she be honest — without losing Michael?

Look out for Roswell High #7
The Vanished
Coming soon from Pocket Books!

FEARLESS™

. . . a girl born without the fear gene

Seventeen-year-old Gaia Moore is not your typical
high school senior. She is a black belt in karate, was
doing advanced maths in junior school and, oh yes,
she absolutely Does Not Care. About anything. Her
mother is dead and her father, a covert anti-terrorist
agent, abandoned her years ago. But before he did,
he taught her self-preservation. Tom Moore knew
there would be a lot of people after Gaia because of
who, and what, she is. Gaia is genetically enhanced
not to feel fear and her life has suddenly become
dangerous. Her world is about to explode with ter-
rorists, government spies and psychos bent on taking
her apart. But Gaia does not care. She is Fearless.